Carn

Patrick McCabe was born in County Monaghan, Ireland,
in 1955. He has published a children's story, *The Adven-
tures of Shay Mouse* (1985), and two other adult novels,
Music on Clinton Street (1986) and *The Dead School*
(1995). *The Butcher Boy* was the winner of the *Irish
Times*/Aer Lingus Literature Prize 1992 and was short-
listed for the 1992 Booker Prize. His play *Frank Pig Says
Hello*, based on *The Butcher Boy*, was first performed at
the Dublin Festival in 1992. He lives in Dublin with his
wife and two daughters.

Also by Patrick McCabe in Picador

THE BUTCHER BOY
THE DEAD SCHOOL

Carn

Patrick McCabe

PICADOR

First published 1989 by Aidan Ellis Publishing Limited

This edition published 1993 by Picador
an imprint of Macmillan Publishers Ltd
25 Eccleston Place, London SW1W 9NF
and Basingstoke

Associated companies throughout the world

ISBN 0 330 32808 5

5 7 9 8 6 4

A CIP catalogue record for this book is available from
the British Library.

Phototypeset by AKM Associates (UK) Ltd, London
Printed and bound in Great Britain by
Mackays of Chatham PLC, Chatham, Kent

The author would like to express his thanks to the Tyrone Guthrie Centre, Annaghmakerrig, where some of this book was written.

To Dympna and Bernard McCabe

Part One

I

The night the railway closed.

That was the night the clock stopped in the town of Carn, half a mile from the Irish border.

For over a hundred years, the black steam engines with their tails of smog had hissed into the depot at the edge of the town.

It was inconceivable that it would ever be any other way.

So when the official from the headquarters of the Great Northern Railway arrived to address the assembled employees, they were somewhat taken aback by his frosty detachment. "Do you realise?" he said, "that there are as many passengers using this line now as there were a hundred years ago?"

He went on to read them lists of percentages and figures, quoting from various complex documents. They looked at him open-mouthed. Then he removed his spectacles and said, "We are left with little choice but to close down the branch line in Carn." He said that they greatly regretted the decision but it had been given very careful thought and it had been decided that there was no other possible course of action. Then he said goodbye and was gone.

The workers were stunned. They cursed and swore and went from that to reason and desperation and how to cut costs. They stayed in the Railway Hotel bar until the small hours, but the more they argued and debated the more-helpless they felt. They went over his words again and again. And the more they repeated them, the more they realised how serious he was. By the time they emerged into the light of the morning, it had well and truly sunk in.

By the end of 1959, there would be no railway in the town of Carn.

After that, all talk of the railway began to gradually recede and after a while it was as if it had never existed. The place went to rack and ruin. Within a matter of weeks, the town plummeted from aristocrat to derelict. Under cover of darkness, rocks were hurled through the windows of the depot. Sleepers were torn up and used to make garden fences, or simply left to rot on waste ground. Paint peeled off doors. Many of the workers emigrated to England and America, standing with their suitcases on The Diamond, waiting for the bus to take them to the ferry terminals of Dublin and Belfast. Those who remained loitered at the street corners, dividing their time between the bookmaker's and the public house. They turned away sourly from each other and looked up and down the deserted main street. It got to the stage where no one expected anything good to happen ever again. It might happen elsewhere, but it would not happen in Carn. Not as far as they were concerned.

Above the jeweller's shop the clock stood still at three o'clock and nobody bothered to fix it—and that was the way it stayed for a long time.

On a warm summer's evening in 1965, when James Cooney, formerly of The Terrace, Carn, drove his Zephyr down the main street of the town, he could not believe his eyes. He stared aghast at the dilapidated shopfronts and the cluster of lethargic layabouts at the corner, at the broken pump skitting its umbrella of water all over the cracked paving slabs. He shook his head and turned the car towards the outskirts where he had just bought a new bungalow. As he lay in bed that night, his mind was whirring with schemes and possibilities.

At fifty years of age, he knew now, he hadn't even started.

It was not long before the citizens of Carn began to notice the imposing figure of James Cooney. They remembered him as a quiet retiring youth who had worn his brother's trousers three sizes too big for him and carted offal from the abattoir in a zinc bucket. They found it hard to reconcile their hazy memories of him with the confident strut of the man who now walked the streets daily. They assumed he was on holiday.

But it soon became apparent that James Cooney was on no holiday. His wife and children were installed lock stock and barrel in the bungalow. James Cooney had come to stay.

He's mad, they said.

He'll rue the day he left America or England or wherever the hell he was to come back here to this kip. Godforsaken hole. Someone suggested that he had been run out of America. "I'd like to know what has him here all the same," said another.

It was not long however before news of his intentions reached their ears.

A factory? they said. Then they shook their heads. It won't work. Look at the railway.

In the bars, former classmates said of him, "Who does he think he is? I remember Mr Clarke booting him around the classroom. He couldn't add two and two." Many of them vowed to have nothing whatever to do with his projects. They weren't going to be caught out twice. They would show James Cooney they weren't born yesterday. They were no fools.

But James didn't mind. He just shrugged his shoulders and looked elsewhere for assistance. It didn't take him long to realise that there were many in the neighbouring towns across the border who would be more than willing to give him all the help they could.

And when the skeleton of metal girders appeared on the skyline, erected by northmen who crossed the border enthusiastically in their cars every day, the most vehement opponents of James Cooney began to re-assess their position. As the building went on and the structure took shape, the people began to regret their lack of co-operation. Their sons and daughters became impatient when they saw the northmen drinking in the public houses. There was nothing they could do but swallow their pride. To cover their tracks they began to praise James Cooney from the heights. They said he had been the best pupil ever in the primary school. They invented stories of his childhood enterprise and industry. They claimed that his good fortune abroad had come as no surprise to them. Then they packed off their children to the factory where the neon letters CARN MEAT PROCESSING PLANT rose boldly over the meagre rooftops of the town.

The streets filled up with cars. Workers thronged the square and The Diamond at lunch hour. The plant horn hooted every morning as if to say, "Wake up Carn!"

The jeweller's clock had to be fixed so that the workers could be back in time after lunch. James Cooney called them all by their Christian names and winked intimately at them as he passed by on the factory floor. He gave them bonuses for extra effort so that by the time the factory had been in operation a mere year the workers were so absorbed in their work the only people left who cared anything for the railway or even the memory of it were the old people with one foot in the grave.

After he had crossed that hurdle, it was a clear run for

James Cooney. He seemed to be everywhere at once. He organised festivals and opened them himself. His photograph stared almost every week from the front page of the local newspaper. He became president of numerous societies and chairman of the council. All in the space of one year. It seemed that from deep inside his bungalow on the edge of town he was transmitting atomic energy that was rapidly changing everything for miles around.

Having observed the success of James Cooney, a teenage girl just out of school rented a premises for herself and filled it with clothes she had bought in the city. Above the door she painted a sign in crazy whorled lettering: "She-Gear for She-Girls!" Then a television shop opened up offering attractive rental rates and in no time at all the humdrum daily conversation had been invaded and supplanted by the interweaving plots of American soap operas.

A businessman from across the border moved into town and set up a supermarket, the like of which had never been seen before in the county not to mention the town. Vast lettering promised ridiculous knock-down bargains. THE FIVE-STAR SUPERMARKET it was called. Its proprietor, a mild-mannered man with a soft northern voice, got to know all the locals by name and slipped many of them small presents with their first orders. His name was Alec Hamilton and before long, they were speaking of him as if he and all belonging to him had been living in the town for generations. The supermarket became the most popular shopping centre for miles around.

But not to be outdone, James set his wheels in

motion once more. He purchased the run-down parish hall, painted it a garish pink and completely refurbished its interior. He fixed a giant imitation precious stone above the door. This premises became known as THE SAPPHIRE BALLROOM. Where once shy young couples had jigged to the sound of an accordeon band, now abrasive youths aped dance crazes from England and America. Bikers from northern towns loitered at the back of the hall. The dancers hung about the streets until all hours singing and cheering, then parped their car horns noisily all the way home.

James Cooney's appetite was well and truly whetted by the success of his dance hall venture. He purred inwardly when it was said to him, "Just how do you do it?" Other businessmen felt three inches tall beside him.

It was to put himself out in front once and for all that he decided to build the Turnpike Inn. On his way home from one of his routine visits to the factory he dropped into a hostelry, ostensibly to have a bottle of stout but in fact to put a proposition to the grey-haired owner with the white apron. When he heard what James had to say, the owner screwed up his face and muttered to himself saying, "I don't know Mr Cooney." But James Cooney's time in Boston and New York had taught him nothing if not persistence so day after day he haunted the place until the owner's spidery signature went on the piece of paper that he produced from his pocket. When the owner went out to tell his wife, James Cooney had a good look at his new acquisition. The smell from the outside toilet wafted to his nostrils. Slops dripped indolently on to the sticky tiles. "Jee-zus," he said under his breath.

Not long afterwards, the JCB crawled up the main street like a prehistoric beast. It took one step back and then one forward and when it retreated again, half the wall was gone. It didn't take very long to get rid of the rest. Some of the old people who were watching felt as if lumps of themselves were being wrenched away. Rumours spread like wildfire through the factory. Exotic nights of drinkfilled promise appeared before the workers. The other publicans cursed him. But nothing would stop him now. He had been quick to notice the change in the people since he had built the meat plant and given them money for their televisions and records and fridge-freezers and clothes. He knew the eagerness with which they watched detectives from the Bronx roar down highways bigger than any roads they had ever seen in their lives. He monitored their speech which took its cue from the soap operas and the songs. That said something to James and his days in the Big Apple had left him well-equipped to deal with it.

He lay awake at night with names racing through his head, highways and skyscrapers and skating waitresses merging into each other. Then one night he jumped up suddenly in bed and his wife grabbed him as if he was making a suicide leap.

"The Turnpike Inn," he cried triumphantly.

The minister who came to cut the tape stood in the midday sunshine smiling at everyone and tapping ash on to the mud the JCB had left behind. His stomach slumped over his belt in despair, haplessly restrained by his striped nylon shirt. He drummed on his lapels with his fingers and waited for the people to ask him questions. When nobody asked anything because they were too stunned by the speed with which James Cooney had completed the whole thing, the minister went on to make a speech. It started off being about Carn and the great railway junction it had been but it went on to being about James Cooney. Men like him were the future of the country, he said. He gestured towards the Turnpike Inn. "A short time ago," he continued, "this was just a small, pokey little—no offence to the previous owner—smalltown bar. And now it is a thriving modern tavern-cum-roadhouse which will give employment to . . ." He leaned over and whispered to James. "To ten people," he went on. "This is indeed a marvellous achievement. Carn has come a long way in the past couple of years and long may this progress continue. With men like James Cooney here, we need have no fear ladies and gentlemen that it will. I now pronounce the Turnpike Inn formally open!"

The sound of clapping filled the air as he cut the tape and when the furore was abating a woman tugged at his sleeve and asked him would there be any chance of a council house.

Half the town surged inside and marvelled at what lay before them. John F. Kennedy and Davy Crockett stared at them from the red-velveted walls. Two

American flags criss-crossed on the ceiling. Bar-becued chickens turned slowly on a spit behind glass. In an alcove a monochromatic Manhattan skyline stretched upwards. The drinkers gawped at the vastness of the lounge bar with its sepia photograph of a market day in the thirties which took up most of one wall. They sank into plush seats and stared at the rickety carts and herded beasts, perplexed. They kept waiting for some figure of authority to come along and tap them on the shoulder, ordering them to move along. But nobody did any such thing. They stayed there until closing time and when they found them-selves standing half-dazed in the main street, they swore they would never drink in any other pub in the town of Carn as long as they lived. They raised uncertain thumbs upwards and tried to focus as they shouted at the blue moon hanging above the railway, "James Cooney has done it again! He's gone and done it again!"

After that the Turnpike Inn became the focal point of the community. Many groups came from neigh-bouring towns to hold their meetings in the lounge and the function room. Public representatives hired out rooms on a regular basis. Older men left the grey interiors of bars they had frequented all their lives and came to sit with the eclectic clientele in the bright light of the lounge bar, the sudden gunshots on the television and the smell of cooking food not seeming to bother them at all. The middle-aged men who had previously confined themselves to the dark, anony-mous corners of the hotels, now ventured forth with their wives who sat nervously beside them.

That was the town in the year 1966. The old people staring at the wreckage of broken beer bottles and squashed chip bags on the streets outside the Turnpike Inn and the Palace Cinema (recently renovated and its display case adorned with a woman around whose half-naked frame the words MONDO BIZARRE curled provocatively), lying awake at night as the men in the sequinned suits tuned up their guitars in The Sapphire, wringing their hands and feeling that their time had prematurely come as the young people pushed brusquely past them as if to say, "There's damn all you can do it about now. Why don't you go off and tell some fool the story of the railway?"

And James Cooney stood in the doorway of the Turnpike Inn thinking of the day he left with his gaberdine and his suitcase in spite of all the locals who had vehemently dissuaded him with graphic tales of misfortune in the predatory streets of New York. He shook his head and smiled to himself before going inside to finalise the arrangements for the Take Your Pick competition which would have them packing in any time after eight.

II

The Dolans were well known in the town of Carn. Matt Dolan had been shot dead in a raid on the railway in 1922. His name was revered. The school-master in Benny Dolan's class referred to him as "Carn's true hero".

But there were others who were not so sure. Benny first became aware of this the night the custom-hut outside Carn was blown up. Late that night when he was in bed, he heard voices downstairs and thought perhaps it was his uncles who occasionally visited at a late hour but, as he stood on the landing deciphering, he realised that they were voices he had never heard before. And when he saw the policeman holding his father by the arm and leading him towards the door, his first instinct was to cry out but he could not. When the door had closed behind them, he ran downstairs to his mother and asked her, ma why did they do it? But she just held him and kept repeating, "He didn't do it son, he didn't do it. They want him for everything that's done son, they can't leave him alone."

In the newspaper the following day there was a photograph of the blackened shell of the custom-post. Above it in large black type IRA ATTACK BORDER POST.

When Benny's father came home three days later, the uncles arrived late in the night. They stayed until the small hours conversing in taut whispers. Benny's father related his experiences in the police station in slow, deliberate tones. They had been watching him, they said. That he had met men from across the border. Northmen. They had information, they said. Why couldn't he sign the confession? It would go easier on him in the long run. The knuckles of his uncles whitened as they drank in every syllable. The fire flickered on their faces as they drew in closer to share it with him. It was light when he had finished his tale. The uncles stood in the doorway and gripped his hand warmly. "You're one of the best," they said to him. Then they set off down the road to catch the morning train to Derry. Benny Dolan didn't sleep a wink after that, his dreams filled with burning custom-posts and running men, sudden cries at the back of his mind.

After that, he became a hero in his class. He led schoolboy expeditions to the border where the northern police patrolled with tracker dogs. In the games after that, the blowing of bridges and the storming of custom-huts were incorporated with enthusiasm. They scanned daily papers for photographs and varied their make-believe exploits with each new development.

When two IRA volunteers were riddled with bullets outside the town in September 1958, the boys worked themselves into a frenzy. They swore that they would invade Northern Ireland and kill all the protestants. They would murder all the policemen. No military personnel would be spared. They listened feverishly as the details of the barracks raid were related over and over again in the houses. The lorry had driven past the barracks by mistake and then reversed. A grenade had been flung and bounced back off the door, rolling in underneath the lorry. It had exploded and written off the vehicle, the barracks remaining unscathed. Two of the volunteers, one a popular man who sold vegetables from door to door, had fled for their lives and made it to within feet of the southern side of the border where they had been cornered by police and B-Specials. They had pinned them up against the wall of a barn and sprayed them with machine-gun fire. They had left them lying in their own blood. None of the boys could sleep much that night, thinking of the young man, not much older than themselves, staring out of dead eyes in a deserted barn in South Fermanagh, his head limp on his shoulders like a rag doll's. Benny Dolan twisted and turned the whole night long.

The funeral cortege passed through the silent streets of the town. The Dead March played from an open window as the coffin was eased into the grave. The Last Post was sounded by a lone bugler from the brass band. Benny felt his stomach turning over. The funeral was reported on the evening news and Benny's father listened to it with his fist clenched. The town felt as if it was about to come apart with anger.

For weeks afterwards, the teacher spoke about the

two gallant young men who had been done to death by the authorities in the north. He took out some old copybooks which he had preserved for posterity because of their excellence. He passed them around and read selections of poetry to the astounded students. They had been written as a boy by the youngest of the dead men. The students listened, aghast. They could not believe that someone who had been shot dead on a raiding mission had once sat in the same desks as themselves. They clenched their fists and became red-cheeked like their fathers. The teacher's voice trembled.

But it did not last. A few weeks later, the frenzy had died down and people went about their daily tasks as before. Very slowly all trace of the event passed away.

Then something happened that was to change the atmosphere in the Dolan house for a long time to come. Little more than a year after the death of the volunteers, Benny was wakened in the night by the sound of his parents' voices downstairs. He stood at the top of the stairs and felt the blood drain from his face when he found himself confronted by the sight of his father standing in the hall. There was blood on his trouser leg and his face was dirt-caked. Benny's mother was trying to calm him down but he kept ranting about something and made no sense. "It's all right," Benny's mother repeated, "it's all right Hugo." When he saw the tears in his father's eyes, Benny was shocked, it sent a dart of anxiety to his stomach. "It all went wrong," he said. "Joe's shot. I had to leave him Annie. They got Joe. We—we blew the wall. But there was three of them upstairs. We called on them to surrender. They weren't supposed to be there—they came down firing. It all went wrong. I don't know how it happened. Oh Christ . . ."

Benny went back to his room, his heart racing. All night long he waited for the sound of the police hammering on the front door. But it did not come.

In the days that followed, Benny's father did not leave the house. He sat from early morning staring into the dead ashes of the firegrate, cups of tea going cold on the arm of the chair. The abortive raid was reported in the newspapers, along with photographs of Joe Carron, one of the raiders who had been wounded in the attack and later died.

When people came to the house now there was no longer any chatter. Nobody knew what to do because Hugo Dolan would not talk to anyone. He just sat staring into the fire, his face grey. When they said, "Joe Carron died a good man," he looked up with eyes that had no feeling in them. When they castigated the institutions of Northern Ireland, he did not reply, their animation followed by cavernous silences.

Even when, the following year, the IRA formally announced the cessation of its activities along the border, Benny's father made no reference to it. When he came in from work, he sat in the armchair with his eyelids drooping, speaking only of the weather and the course of his business. News items which before would have halted all activity in the kitchen now drifted past anonymously.

The time passed and the people of Carn forgot there had ever been any trouble along the border. The empty shell of the custom-post was bulldozed and a new building erected in its place. The blown bridges were rebuilt, the southern police and army were withdrawn. The customs men began to smile again and tilted their harp-badged white caps as they chatted leisurely to the drivers. It all became the colour of an old photograph, fading by day as the new prosperity encroached upon the town of Carn.

In Benny Dolan's classroom, a portrait of the dead volunteer gathered dust in a corner, his copybook poetry lay forgotten in an ink cupboard.

When Benny was in his final year at the vocational school, aged 16, there was an announcement that the town was to commemorate the fiftieth anniversary of the 1916 rising and the Junior Chamber of Commerce had decided to erect a plaque in the town square to the memory of Commandant Matt Dolan who had led the raid on the railway in 1922. Furthermore, the town square, which was then called Carn Square, was to be renamed Dolan Square.

Tricoloured posters appeared all over the town. Above the new record shop (a recent addition to the Trendy Boutique) a speaker blared martial tunes. Young children once more set about making rifles and assembling gangs. The library set up an exhibition of photographs of the insurrection. Buildings burned everywhere and khaki men raced through rubble and devastated city streets. Machine-guns rat-tat-tatted on the radio as the Dublin of 1916 caved in on itself. The Sapphire Ballroom was transformed into a theatre where the local people performed their version of that Easter's events. The Turnpike Inn resounded with songs of the rebellion, James Cooney obliging with a song of his father's endeavouring as best he could to mask all trace of his American accent as he sang. Eyes fell and ribs were nudged as he raised his fist and brought them all with him—oh what matter when for Ireland dear we fall.

The new plaque was draped in green and gold.

The day of the unveiling of the plaque Carn Sons of St Patrick marched through the streets with their green and gold banner held high, the bass drum booming. Benny's father had consented to being guest of honour on account of his own father, and now stood nervously beside the minister who checked his notes and straightened his tie. Then he began to speak. "The day has not yet come in which we can write the epitaph of Robert Emmet. It has not come because the Ireland that he wished for, the Ireland in which differences between sections of our people would have been forgotten—that day has not yet arrived . . ."

He went on in that vein for over half an hour. Then he said he would like to call on Hugo Dolan to assist him in the unveiling of the plaque. A loud cheer went up from the crowd. Aware of the discomfort of the police who flanked him, in particular the detective whose duty it had been some years before to arrest him, Hugo Dolan smiled as he shook the hand of the minister. Benny felt a surge of pride as he listened to his father speak of that fateful day in 1922, of the hunger that had been in Matt Dolan to see the country free, a hunger that he himself had always understood and shared. Men said to each other in the crowd, "It's the same old Hugo all right. You don't put men like him down so easy . . ." When the speeches were over, the crowd clapped and moved back as the ritual began. There was a roll of drums as the national flag was lowered to half-mast. The crowd scanned the sky as if they expected it to darken. The minister moved forward facing the plaque on the wall. He tugged at the cord and the velvet curtain rolled back. The band played a slow air. "Erected to the memory of Commandant Matt Dolan, North Monaghan Brigade, IRA, Killed In Action 1922 . . ." read the minister over a whistling microphone. The crowd cheered again and banjos and accordeons struck up a tune on the stage with local musicians winking at their families who waved proudly up at them. After a time, the people began to disperse and drift in the direction of the taverns and hotels, and Benny for the first time drank a number of bottles of stout which were bought for him by men who told him that the name of Dolan had gone down in history. One man dragged long and hard on his cigarette and whispered out of the side of his mouth, "Your grandfather took a bullet in the head. He died a soldier. My own father was at the funeral. And that man there, your own father, he got it from them too, both sides of the fence, our own free state lackies and all, they gave him the treatment. That's your breed son. And I hope you're made of the same stuff. I know you are."

The alcohol was taking effect and Benny did not reply to any of this as he was having difficulty focussing on the words, the movement of the man's lips capturing his whole attention. A group in the corner demanded silence. From their mouths uncoiled a lament for Ireland's division. Then someone stood on a chair and called for three cheers for Hugo Dolan. When Benny heard the name he tried to wade his way back through the fog that the drink had drawn about his mind but the volume of the cry they sent up confused him even more. It was only when he saw the glass shaking in his father's hand that things began to clear for Benny. When the cheer had subsided they all looked expectantly at Hugo Dolan. They were sure that the smile they wanted would soon spread across his face. But it did not. And when he spat and flung the glass against the wall where it smashed in pieces, they were dismayed. They looked at him, awaiting his explanation. His hands trembled. "Fucking circus," he said tensely. "Fancy flags and a porter-bellied minister wining it above in the hotel with the doctor and the priest. They get their rewards all right. They'll see to themselves. The same people who locked up Luke Devlin and Mickey Kerr, parading like fucking royalty. Off to Dublin with the Thompson Gun. Fighting the good fight. The hand on the shoulder boys—I'm with you all the way men. Up the republic. Let them ask Joe Carron about the republic, or Lukey, twenty years in front of him. Hypocrites and liars! A bunch of mealy-mouthed sham republicans! Republic—don't make me fucking laugh!"

They stared at him in disbelief and wondered what to do next. They looked away and hoped he would disappear. He swayed to and fro and stared. Then he turned on his heel and left, banging the door behind him. The humming began anew and they turned to the bar, splitting up into various groups to discuss this sensational new development. Some of them attributed it to nervous trouble that he had never got over. He had seen them being riddled. "How would you get over that?" they asked. Others felt that this wasn't true. They said that Hugo Dolan had always been a bit touchy. They recalled incidents which although innocuous at the time now appeared loaded with significance. They continued to drink and debate, their initial understanding and objectivity gradually being overtaken by anger and annoyance. It began to seem as if Hugo Dolan had spoiled the whole day for everyone. They said that no matter what trouble he had had himself he had no business going about insulting the people of the town. And the minister, that minister had done a lot for Carn. It was he who had tried to step in and block the closing of the railway. One man suggested that they ought to break the newly-erected plaque to teach Dolan a lesson.

The debate was still raging when Benny finished his drink and went outside.

He stood in the doorway to get his bearings. Above the town hall the tricolour sagged. The signatories of 1916 stared impassively from the library window. Benny stood there, replaying the hurt and anger on his father's face. Then, hearing new voices in the yard behind him, he set off across the empty square towards home.

III

The day the Turnpike Inn opened its doors to the goggle-eyed citizens of Carn, Sadie Rooney leaned over the privet hedge at the bottom of her garden and thought to herself how much she loved Elvis Presley. She would have gone anywhere with him and indeed dreamed up an interminable series of locations where herself and the handsome crooner tripped the light fantastic. Fairgrounds where they soared into the vast blueness of the sky on the back of a big dipper to the accompaniment of a pulsating rock and roll sound-track. The very mention of the word "Elvis" made every muscle in her body stiffen. Whenever an Elvis film was due to play in the local cinema, she was tense for days before. She knew every line of dialogue in *Love Me Tender* and whenever she got the chance would relate the entire plot from beginning to end. She would savour every moment and work herself into a frenzy until tears came to her eyes as she spoke of the bullets hitting Elvis as he lay dying on the prairie with his guitar beside him. She spent her Saturdays locked in her room with stacks of his singles which she played repeatedly. Since she had begun to earn money of her own in Carn Poultry Products, her bedroom had become awash with colour. Cross-channel pop stars and Irish showbands covered every available inch of wallpaper. The St Martin De Porres picture which Father John had sent over from Kenya was barely visible. This didn't please Sadie's mother at all. She had been brooding over it for a long time. She felt that to have a holy man like St Martin in such dubious company was not right. She confronted her daughter and said, "It's time you quit all this, the filth and dirt of the day put into your head by the likes of that Una Lacey one above in the factory." But this made no impression on Sadie who had been quietly coming to the conclusion that if she was paying for her keep she had her rights too. So between herself and her mother there developed a tension which manifested itself in the flick of teacloths and sudden coughs. Finally one day her mother, tormented by a large fuel bill and the muddy boots of her husband, stormed into her room and cried, "You'll not ignore me. I didn't wash floors on my hands and knees, scrubbing out that kip of a school for fifteen years just to have the likes of you turn around and laugh at me. I'm fed up being walked on by you and him!" Then she set about tearing every picture in the room and didn't stop until the wall was bare.

"Maybe that will put a bit of manners on you now," she said, whitefaced. "Maybe now you'll listen to me." Then she stormed out, stunned by the depth of her own fury.

Sadie threw herself on the bedspread as she had seen them do in the magazines and films and pummelled the pillows bitterly. When the light had faded and a calm had at last descended, she managed to stir herself to gather up the remnants of a sorry-looking beach boys and dickybowed songsters. She had a restive sleep that night but in the days that followed, when her mother had pulled in her horns and reverted to her more traditional sullenness, Sadie set about rebuilding the wreckage and applied herself with diligence to the task. And no less than a week later, all were back in business, pouting and crooning and strutting for all they were worth.

St Martin de Porres looked down as she flicked through *True Romance Tales* and dickeyed her hair up like the girls in the magazine. Her bedroom became a sort of theatre where all manner of fantasy popped out of her head and came alive. Sadie really wanted to be one of the girls in the magazine. The more she became familiar with their lifestyles, the more she became disgusted with the smell of chickens' innards and the bloodstained overall she had to wash every night. She practised the way the girls walked, stepping back and forward in front of the bedroom mirror. She invented men in silk suits who came out of the same mirror and said to her, "Would you like to dawns?" There was no question of any of these men speaking in local dialect. They drove MG cars and took her for drinks in bars with brass pump handles and pictures of race horses. The magazine girls lay around all day doing each others' hair and talking about "someone special". Hearts came out of their mouths when they spoke about him. They said he was a "dream". They said he was "fab". When he came into the story in person he was usually a complete stranger in town. He had dark hair and a plaid jacket. He rarely spoke, but anything that came out of his lantern jaw was noted by the girls. There was always one of them lurking nearby. They trailed him and found out what kind of books he liked. Then they went and read those kind of books hoping they would get the chance to say something to him about them. They found out where he had his dinner too. Then they turned up there as well. Sometimes he gave them a distant smile across his newspaper. That drove them distracted. They argued among themselves which girl he liked the best. His arrival threatened to shatter the harmony which had previously existed in the flat. He was never a dustbin man or anything like that. Sometimes an antique dealer or record producer or big time insurance man. An odd time it turned out he was married. Just near the end of the story one of the girls would see this one in a feather boa taking his arm in the hotel foyer and then she'd spot the ring. This was the end of the world for the girls. They left their clothes lying in disarray around the flat and picked on each other for no reason, staring moonily out of the window chewing emery boards and twirling beads. Or another time he might make it his business to get to know the least pushy girl, the one that wasn't quite as up to date as the rest. This was equally bad for they turned on her then. *How dare she? She should never have been in the flat in the first place,* they said. But all that didn't matter for he didn't marry any of them anyway.

They were always to be seen in the last frame swopping handkerchiefs by the dozen and asking themselves why oh why oh why.

Then off he drove in his MG with his pipe stuck in his gob.

But men such as this never seemed to include the town of Carn on their itinerary. In any case no MG was ever to be seen parked outside the Golden Chip café which was the stomping ground of the town's male inhabitants. It was there Sadie Rooney spent her Saturday nights after she had the rows with her mother, hunched over coffee cups and drawing shapes in the smoke. There was bubbling fat and formica and the girls from The Park and Jubilee Terrace draped over the jukebox singing. They whispered among themselves, "We will get a man. And his name will be Julio. Or Clint. Or Jeff. And he will bring us to his beach house. To his beach house with French windows." They spoke in asthmatic gasps about dreamboats and dishes. Every Saturday they scrubbed the smell of chickens from them, then ensconced themselves beneath the picture of Florence in the corner of the café, plucking hairs off Paul McCartney's jacket, twisting on the tiles with Wayne Fontana and Scott Walker, one dream trying to outdo the next.

—The races for me. That's where I'm going.
—He'll bring you? He will in his eye.
—Yes he will he will he will.
—A hacienda for me. Oh I can hardly wait.
—A hacienda with Julio.
—A heart-shaped pool.

—With Julio?
—With anyone.
—Los Angeles for me, The City of Angels.
—The Palais A-Go Go!
—We will do the bossa nova!
—The Hippy Shake Shake!
—These bloody streets!
—Farrell the foreman!
—Have youse them packed yet, girls?
—Yes Mr Farrell.
—No Mr Farrell.
—Go to hell Mr Farrell.
—Damned rain!
—Empty streets!
—Damned rain!
—And Barney The Buck with his hand on his—
—Quit!

Then, as every Saturday, after the initial euphoria had worn off, they settled back to lethargy as they stared at the melting colours on the neon flower that was the centrepiece of the jukebox. And across from them, eyes sized up their bodies over the rims of teacups, male fingers tapped ash and dredged their flesh hungrily. *The Single Girls Needs A Sweet Lovin' Man to Lean On*, sang Sandy Posey. As far as the huddled male youths in the corner were concerned, any one of their number would have been more than willing to oblige with a few extras thrown in for good measure. They pulled on their cigarettes and tightened sweaty brows.

—Would I, they said, would I what.
—Would ya boy, by Jazus I would.

—The lamps on that.

—The one in the red.

—The one in the blue.

—Hold me back hold me back.

—All the way and back for more, boys.

They stubbed their cigarettes in the tray with a vengeance. As Sandy Posey took her leave and the record twisted back inwards, the girls looked up to see Francie Mohan making his Saturday night speech, dead on time, nine-thirty, five minutes after his ejection from the Railway Hotel where he had been drinking all day having slipped in for a quiet beer, leaving the Sunday dinner strapped to the carrier of his Humber bicycle which would lie against the gable end of the pub until Monday when his wife would beat him in to retrieve it, or what was left of it after the tinkers and the dogs had finished with it. He brought the girls out of their trance and gave the men a cosy smirk for themselves as they lit fresh cigarettes and prepared to enjoy to the full what they had heard a hundred times. Francie raised a single unsteady hand and demanded attention from one and all.

"In nineteen twenty-two they shot Matt Dolan. The scum of British jails with a ticket from the king to kill all before them, and that's what they did to poor Matt, left him lying above at the railway in his own red blood.

"But now there's no more of that, no sir. They took the boat, aye one and all and it was Fermanagh the rebel county that put the run on them. They showed Perfidious Albion where to get off. So now they've gone lock stock and barrel only for the six wee counties up the road and we'll get them back any day now. The Fenian can hold his head up with the best of them. Now he can look the world full square in the teeth. I have two buck goats, four walls of my own two miles outside this town, what more do I want? Isn't that right, lads?"

He twirled a Players and looked through one end of it like a telescope. "Never got nothing by lying down, isn't that right, lads? How much is a bag of chips?"

"One and six small, two and six large," said Sergio of the blue nylon coat tiredly and looked away as he dug deeper in the churning grease.

One eye went into a slit and Francie fumbled for the imaginary revolver that had served him well in the troubled times. "What? What? Two and what? Robbers! Rogues and robbers! Where are you from? Roma? Roma! Three coins in the fountain! You'll not rob Francie! Francie can put it up to the eyeties! Any ten of you!"

Then he went down like a sack of potatoes, snug as a bug on the grease-caked tiles. Men in green uniforms and bandoliers pack-drilled through his dreams.

And after all was over, Sadie Rooney the single girl walked home alone, deep in her handbag an arc of hearts curling from the supine head of a blonde who swooned into the arms of the rugged MG driver who momentarily removed his pipe to kiss her. For a brief moment she saw her own features on the face of the girl. As she passed the abattoir on the square, she conjured up swaying palms for herself but the broken fence rattling in the ditch shook her out of her reverie. A stray terrier sniffed at her ankle and she cursed bitterly as she asked herself why oh why was she born at the back end of the world to hook the anaemic legs of chickens and turkeys for the likes of Farrell the foreman with his bloodstained clipboard and his beady eye, to spend her evenings in Jubilee Terrace elbow deep in stewed washing, her scowling mother hovering over her with a pocketful of clothes pegs and a barb for every occasion, tales by the score of possibility thwarted. It's all right for Sandy Posey, she sings of the single girl all alone in the bedsits of London but she knows that outside her window any time she wants the yellow lights will wink with promise, radios play through the night and the odd sports car stop outside. But here—Carn? The howl of dogs, the rattle of tin and a crabbed mother rotting in the chimney corner with fingers like sticks.

She looked up to see her neighbour Mr Galvin doffing his cap as he wheeled his bicycle past.

"Not too bad of a night," he said. "I thought it was going to turn out a bit colder."

"Yes Mr Galvin," replied Sadie, "warm enough now."

Mr Galvin lived in number four and ever since her days of cut knees her prevailing image of him had been that of a cocked backside above a pile of manure. Mr Galvin and his garden, man and wife. He loved his ridges more than his real wife. Ridges and manure and a little garden fork.

Christ Jesus, thought Sadie, I wonder does our Sandy tend her ridges in London? The smell of manure in Croydon. Oh I'll get away from this godforsaken hole yet, I'll not die here an old biddy with veins and a teapot and hair like wire. 'Ello Mr Galvin, just got 'ome, didn't I? How are your sweet peas coming along? Climbing up the trellis okay?

Sadie smiled as she saw him in her mind, doffing his cap and searching its fabric for an appropriate response.

—Oh aye Sadie, climbing, climbing sure enough, no trouble with the sweet pea but there's damn the sign of the lettuce. I wonder did the grubs get at it? Them brown grubs are a curse. Do youse have much trouble with the brown lads Sadie? Eh?

—No, as a matter of fact we don't, said Sadie aloud, to tell you the truth we don't have any grubs at all. No brown grubs. No black grubs. Not a grub in sight. And do you know what Mr Galvin? No ridges either. Nope. Not one.

She saw the disbelief on Mr Galvin's face. He looked at her as if someone dear to him had just been assassinated.

—No, repeated Sadie, no grubs or ridges or manure. I'm a London secretary Mr Galvin. Do you like my Mary Quant dress?

—Oh is that right, replied Mr Gavin, is that right now? God but isn't the world a queer place too? Well I dare say you won't be planting much curly kale in London. Boys oh boys oh boys.

Finishing up her daydream, Sadie watched Mr Galvin as he settled his cap on his head and whistled a little tune as he bent beneath the clouds and went rigid as he spotted a rubbery grub making a bee line for a potato stalk.

—I can't wait, said Sadie, gonna be great, innit? Wotcher, gels? Wayne or Scott around?

"Got you!" cried Mr Galvin as he leaped on the grub squeezing it between forefinger and thumb as Sadie opened the front door and heard her mother's voice squirming out through the yellow bar of light under the kitchen door, *is that you is that you Sadie* and the bus for Croydon took off down the road as the furry slippers padded across the lino and she stood sourfaced as always surveying her daughter up and down as if she had just contracted a foul disease.

For every day was the same in the house for Sadie and her mother and father.

—Have you the tea made? her mother would say, there's more to be done around here than lie about the Golden Chip with Lacey and all the rest of the layabouts. Get that skirt off you and go down on your knees with this rag and you'll find a bucket under the stairs.

Carn Poultry Products took most of her steam away, so often she went to it without a whimper but what it was she wanted to say bubbled away inside her head—Ah to hell with you and your floor and Mr Galvin and his grubs, I'm going to England if it's the last thing I do there's not one of you can stop me, I'll get a ticket and a bus to Euston and the whole lot of you can go to hell.

ROOM TO LET: REASONABLE RENT
YOUNG LADY PREFERRED

—Wouldn't that be nice now, she thought, just the

one wee room, what more would I need, my hair backcombed and a wage packet on Friday for all the mod gear. Dahn the West End. Could I drink? Yes I could. In the Irish Clubs? The Walls of Limerick and Take Me Home to Mayo? Not on your life. Let the chambermaids and the country gawks jive to their hearts content. I'll be in my stripey trousers and knee boots in a club where the lights carry you off into space and that will be the last you'll see of Sadie, gone for good dahn the Old Kent Road.

The sound of her father's key in the lock sent all her thoughts scurrying for cover, gone with the wind like smoke. He stomped across the floor, all the dirt and dust of the town on his dungarees as he hung them up behind the door and whacked his hip with his squashed cap and sucked his Woodbine, the final favour of a condemned man, then thought for ten minutes before saying, "Hardy day."

In the scullery his wife scowled and grudgingly answered him with a curt platerattle, thinking of something bad he'd done years before. Then he closed one eye and covered a coal with a film of spit.

"Hardy day right enough."

She set the plate of beef down in front of him and fled. He rubbed his dirt-caked hands and attacked it like a gorilla.

The lights staccatoed in the River club in Holborn as Sadie saw herself dancing with an accountancy student from Tipperary. He told her he lived with his brother in Camden but he was only biding his time before he got into the big money and what he wouldn't do then.

—And you, he said, where do you live?

—Me? said Sadie, eyeing up his country trousers and pre-war brogues, oh I live with Elvis Presley in 77 Walm Lane, Willesden. And Wayne. And Scott Walker. What do you think of that young man?

—Walker? he replied, did you you say Walker? He wouldn't be from Tipperary town by any chance?

And as she flung the sodden cloth into the black water of the slop bucket, Sadie looked all around her in despair. As she lay down in her bed that night she stared at the picture of St Martin de Porres and the 1952 calendar with the faded kitten and the metal-work flowers of the fireplace. She looked up at Elvis in his army khaki and with tears in her eyes she said, *What am I going to do Elvis Aaron Presley Elvis The Pelvis King what am I going to do at all at all.*

She waited and waited but there was nothing, only the wind and not a note from the king, not a single solitary sound.

Then click went the light and out went the moon.

IV

The Easter Commemorations were in full swing when Josie Keenan arrived in her native town all the way from Moss Side, Manchester. For a split second she thought she had made a dreadful mistake and somehow come to the wrong town. She stared in awe at the bunting draped across the street and could not believe her ears when she heard music blaring from a speaker above a record shop. She had been expecting the burrowing eyes to fix on her without any delay but the crowds that lined the streets drinking from paper cups and eating chips from newspapers were completely unaware of her presence.

It was only when she lay on her bed in her hotel room that she managed at last to come to terms with the sense of dislocation she was experiencing.

She lay there listening to the sound of the birds twittering outside, in the distance the muffled sound of a bass drum. Far off children's cries echoed and as she drifted towards sleep she saw herself now in that same street, many years before, walking behind her father as he wheezed and bustled ahead of her in his huge belted overcoat, picking her way through the cow pats that dotted the footpath, everywhere the fetid stench of urine. The shanks of beasts rose up above her, she stared in horror at the portwine faces of perplexed farmers who appeared from nowhere in the doorways of public houses.

Her father took her hand, his hard skin rasping against hers like leather. Women in headscarves squeezed fruit and vegetables, squinting suspiciously at the hawkers. The herded beasts stared out helplessly from pens.

She sat with him in the murky interior of a bar where he spat on his hand and slapped another man heartily on the back. The street was deserted as they made their way home. The gate of a makeshift pen rattled idly.

When they reached home, it all began, as before and before that.

"Meat? Call this meat?" he cried. He flung it from him and spat at her. Then he rose and took Josie roughly in his arms. His spiky chin rubbed against her face. "This is my wee woman here," he said, "this is the only woman I care about. Are you my wee girl Josie?" He left her to her bed and the silence took over then. The night hung about Josie as she listened to the moans of her mother in the next room, the bedsprings creaking until there was nothing but the tapping of a branch on the window pane. Josie tried to rub the feel of his spikiness from her face but the more she did the more it spread.

Outside in the square, a loudspeaker announced details of a singing competition which was to take place shortly in the primary school. But Josie's mind could not go back with it or the sound of the voices passing on the street. Her mind went back to him as she watched him blubbering like a child at the open grave, his hands shaking as he cried out, "Cassie, Cassie come back to me, I can't live without you." Neighbour women soothed him, his wild, drink-fired eyes fixed on her and he clutched her by the shoulders, quivering. "What are we going to do now, Josie? How can we manage? She knew how to run everything. I can't be expected to do it, Josie pet, I can't!"

The house fell to decay. Bluemoulded dishes cluttered the sink. Wallpaper peeled and potatoes sprouted on the scullery floor. The collars and cuffs of Josie's favourite dress went black. In the nights he came to her and lifted her from the bed. The drink fumes suffocated her as she felt him draw a line with his finger from her neck to her navel saying, "You always were my pet. You and me miss Cassie. She was an angel, your mother." He nipped her on the neck with his teeth and she felt the race of his heartbeat. Josie did not feel like a human being beneath. She was an inert rag doll. He turned from her and she winced as he spasmed and every nerve in her body tightened as he lay there, crying in the darkness.

When the nurse came and gave her sweets, she brightened and thought of the happy time that the nurse said was coming. She wafted with the stories of pretty dresses and bright airy rooms. The nurse took her hand. She combed her hair gently and said to Josie, "We're going to make you a nice little girl. Little Miss Josephine, that's who you're going to be."

The marble busts stared at Josie with piercing eyes and she walked the corridor with the nun and the huge rooms swept above her and made her dizzy. The room where they slept smelt of horsehair and rough soap and girls her own age looked at her with lifeless eyes. Her days after that became numbed, they fused imperceptibly into each other, measured by the ceaseless, ominous boom of the vast metal bell in the chapel corridor. The tiles echoed with the steady click of spartan heels. The smell of boiling cabbage hung perenially in the air. She curled up at night in a long grey cotton nightdress and sucked her thumb like an infant. The mornings found her in the potato field, bent beneath the sky, her whittled nails ingrained with dirt. Once a magician came and performed tricks with scarves and cardboard tubes but beyond that there was nothing but the icy hand on the wrist and the deadening chant of prayer.

When Josie stood in the doorway of the orphanage for the last time, she turned back and looked at the rows of uncurtained windows set in the granite façade and she thought how much she hated the stifling presence of her own sex. Their body smell, their petulance and finicky moods, their feigned, brittle gentleness. She thought of their scattered clothes on the beds, the relentless exploration of skin in search of new blemishes, their coy deviousness. She never wanted them circling her so closely again.

She found herself standing in Molloy's Select Drapery in the town of Carn and plucked nervously at the buttons of her coat as Molloy pulled the tape measure to and fro on the back of his neck saying, "I don't normally take girls from there you know. It's only on account of the wife and Sister Benignus being so great. She says you're not the worst. I'll tell you this, mind. Any slacking and you're gone. And whatever the wife tells you to do in the kitchen, no mouthing out of you. If you do, there's the door. And no thieving. One thing I can't stand, that's thieving. The wife will give you a shopcoat. Now, away with you. I've work to do. What did you say your name was? Josie?"

She was given her own room with faded wallpaper and a Sacred Heart lamp. A blond Jesus held up two fingers as he looked into Josie's soul and beneath him a small light burned in a scarlet bell jar.

Old women with musty smells tormented her about brassières and corsets.

As time passed, the taint of the orphanage began to leave Josie and when she donned an ice-cream pink mohair sweater, it was not with either shame or fear.

At first when the men came into the shop, her cheeks burned and her hands seemed to take on a life of their own. But the male voices were so different that she could not help following them, her eyes falling to the deep black hairs that covered their hands. She began to realise too that there was something stirring in her and when they stole surreptitious glances at her from behind the suit rack, she pretended not to notice but it filled her with a nervous excitment that all the dead years in the orphanage could not take from her. She lay at night beneath the Sacred Heart lamp and thought of the nun with the bristled chin who for ten years had waved her fist at them ranting and raving about purity and the pale innocent blueness of the virgin.

She thought about the hungry eyes of the men behind the suit rack. She thought about her breasts and wondered what it was that made them want her there. She thought of the girls in the orphanage standing in line at the washbasins, their slack breasts beneath coarse nightdresses. They were breasts. They meant nothing.

What did they mean?

At night Josie painted her fingernails but washed it away the following morning for she had not the courage to face Molloy.

The young man who began to call regularly was not shy like the others. He winked at her from behind the suit rack and once came up to her and said with a grin, "I don't suppose you could tell me where I'd get a pair of socks—I need a pair of socks bad."

Josie had blushed to the roots for she was not quite sure how to deal with this kind of assuredness. But her legs nearly went from under her altogether when he walked into the shop a few days later smoking a cigarette and said to her, "I found out your name—

Josephine." Then he turned and walked out again. He made a few more visits, pretending to inquire about the quality of shirts and jackets but they both knew that they were of no interest to him. His cheekiness made Josie feel warm inside, it was something she had never seen in the orphanage, not once. Women were too afraid, she knew that, they could not have that play in them. None of them wanted to be caught in the spotlight or held up to ridicule. So they trudged along a grey corridor to keep themselves safe.

Josie began to look forward to his visits. When eventually he said, "I bet you didn't know I had a motor car. I think me and you should go for a drive in it. What do you think of that now, Josephine?" Josie did not hesitate for a moment for the excitement was too great inside her and the words just leapfrogged out of her mouth and she said, "Oh, yes."

Every nerve in her body tingled as she got herself ready that Saturday and she pulled on gloves to hide her fingernails, donning the sunglasses when she was well away from Molloy's disapproving eye. She met him outside the town where she found him sitting on a stile. Straight away she blurted out, "That's not a bad day."

He laughed and said, "Do you know something Josephine?"

"What?" replied Josie anxiously.

"You don't even know my name," he said.

Josie felt foolish.

"My name's Culligan. Vinnie Culligan."

Then he put his arm around her and she felt as if the cold hand of the nun had never ever been near her.

They drove to the town of Cavan in his Volkswagen and there they went to the Magnet Cinema where he heaped Scots Clan into her lap and hugged her close to him in the back row. It seemed to Josie that Cavan was on the other side of the world for she had never before been outside her own town. As Navajo Indians swarmed down from the canyon and whooped wildly as they attacked the settlers in their covered wagons, Culligan kissed her ear and she sank into his shoulder. Then he pressed something into her hand and she was afraid to unclasp her fingers. "Go on," he urged. "Open it."

When she saw that it was a small pendant on a chain, her body seemed to melt away; she clutched it tightly until it bit into her palm and she could not get any words to come out of her mouth. She just closed her eyes and wanted that moment never to evaporate for she had never experienced such ecstasy before. After the film they went to the Central Café where their fingers entwined and they listened to songs of love addressed solely to them. She stared lovingly at the smoke that twisted from his cigarette to the yellow ceiling. She felt that no harm could come to her now.

Afterwards they went for a walk along the river bank and just sat watching the current carrying off small sticks and leaves.

"You know something, Josie," Vinne Culligan said, "this should never end."

They met many times after that.

When they went to the guest house, Josie stood by the window staring tensely out into the street, but he acted as if he had known the receptionist all his life. He talked away to her about the hotel business in the nearby towns, they traded neighbours' names and by the time they were done talking there was nothing further from her mind than whether or not they were man and wife. They went upstairs and he threw himself on the bed saying, "Man dear it's great to be young." There was a picture of Maria Goretti on the wall above the bed and beneath it a bunch of dried-out lilac. Outside the dogs barked and the odd passing car threw shadows on the ceiling. Josie lay beside him and as she felt his hand moving along the inside of her thigh she did not care about the pale blue innocent virgin, she wanted them both to melt together and she knew that everything would be all right.

He was quiet on the way back but that was because he was due back at work. They stopped the car a mile from Carn and kissed. It was hard for Josie to believe that a man reared in the town of Carn could talk like Vinnie Culligan.

"I love you so much, Josie," he said to her. She nearly cried when he said it. She took the back lane into town and none of the hawks were any the wiser.

After that, Molloy could not get over the way Josie did her work. And every time Josie thought of Vinnie

Culligan, she fingered the gold pendant nestled beneath her blouse.

She trembled at the thought of the following weekend when he had arranged to call into the shop. When he didn't appear she decided she had picked it up wrongly, that he had meant the following weekend. She waited anxiously that Friday but when the shop closed at nine there was still no sign of him. She cried a little that night and made up all sorts of stories that would excuse him. But then the following Monday it all collapsed when Molloy handed her an envelope and looked at her suspiciously as if he expected her to account for her unauthorised receipt of mail. When eventually he had gone, Josie raced up to her room and when she had picked out the three or four most important words that were half-blurred in front of her eyes, she knew for certain then what the world was all about and she swore bitterly there and then that no one she ever met after that would do the like of it to her again. It was Vinnie Culligan all right. From Wandsworth in England and all he had to say after all they had been through was, "Anything strange?" She went white as a ghost and the room turned over on its side. She kept the letter for weeks hoping that somehow its message would change, that she would one day return to it and find that she had interpreted its message all wrong, that the writing had altered itself and that Culligan was coming to take her with him to England.

But that didn't happen.

What happened was that one day when she was washing her face at the sink she got a terrible wrenching in her stomach and got violently sick. That was the start for Josie Keenan.

That was the start of Culligan's little babby.

She broke a glass vase and tried to cut her wrist with the thick shards but they just wrenched themselves from her hands and she lay on the bed wet-faced and shivering.

As the baby grew within her, she felt as if it were a worm or a serpent. She felt its eerie cackle deep in the pit of her belly.

A long time ago. Days and years ago when the old town of Carn was as it had been for a hundred years before that and never dreamed it would be any different another hundred on.

But it was.

Josie Keenan went to the window and tried to locate the premises of Molloy's Select Drapery.

It was nowhere to be seen.

In its place there was a hairdressing salon and a dry cleaners. It had faded away. And Molloy. And his wife. She felt a dryness coming into her mouth. She could never forget the shop's smell. It came now to her nostrils. And the outline of the dresses on the rails, odd silhouettes hanging in mid-air. Above it all, the moon watching without a word, all that passed, everything that was in her mind. Everything.

All right, thought Josie, *so I buried it. Dug the grave*

all by myself and myself and no Culligan this time, Josie all on her owney-oh, down into the ground it went, into that black hole with the tears running down my face. I didn't want to do it but I did it. It wasn't right what the hell could I have done? I loved it too, I loved its little hands and toes. It had eyes like beads, like a little black lad's it said to me, Don't bury me mammy *but I did. The clay trickled on his cheeks and I filled it in like a madwoman. After that I became as cold as stone and I would have killed Molloy and her and all belonging to them and Culligan and every one of them I ever laid eyes on.*

As she stood by the window, Josie felt the tears coming but she steeled herself against them. She felt the numbness begin in the side of her face. She took three librium tablets from her handbag and sat on the bed with her head buried in her hands.

After that, her mind had not been her own. The voices came to her, sat waiting for her every night in her room. They coiled themselves around her head, the voices of the town and the voices of demons.

Who's that out there on a night like that? Wouldn't you think she'd be foundered with the cold? Wouldn't you now missus? Indeed you would, a night like that would cut you to the bone. What is she at? Bent double beneath the sky. Up to no good I'd swear. Can't be. Look at the face of her. Can't be more than sixteen, shouldn't be let out at this hour never mind . . . what's she doing now—clawing at the clay like a mad thing. Now that's neither right nor normal now is it, I ask you? Oh Jesus Mary and Joseph do you see what she's doing now do you? Look at it, wrapped in a newspaper oh Jesus and his Blessed Mother it's a little child couldn't be more than a day old . . . a little shilde, a little icky babba pale and cold and not a twitch in its bones of course there's madness in her eyes I could tell that from the start, but there's bitches and there's evil bitches . . . let her shake all she likes hanging's too good for a woman would do the like of that, sprinkle clay on a poor ba's face.

The voices crawled all over her and sleep left her. She could not banish the sweats and the headaches. She wanted the people of the town to take her and hang her in the square, but she could not tell them about it. In the small hours of the morning, the voices drove her to the safe where Molloy kept his money and she unrolled several five pound notes from the bundle bound with an elastic band. She hid them under the floorboards in her bedroom, along with knives and forks and assorted pieces of china she had smuggled from the kitchen. Her visits to the safe became more frequent for the voices would not let up. When one night she crept down the stairs pulling her nightgown about her, she felt like breaking down and crying out to Molloy and the people of the town, *Yes I did it I did it* but she did not and when she found herself at that moment standing in the glare of Molloy's flashlight, she did not say anything, she just collapsed into the arms of hopelessness.

Molloy caught her roughly by the shoulder. "You've been leading us a merry dance, my girl. Five nights we've been waiting here for you." His wife peered from the shadows. "Well I'll tell you what you can do. Take us to where you have it. Every last penny of it. Then you can get out on the front street. I should have listened to Kelly—stay well away from that place—they're all wrong ones in there. And that young one's a daughter of the Buyer Keenan that drank himself into the poorhouse. Died roaring. All wrong ones. Or they wouldn't be there."

She removed the floorboard and handed them her treasure trove piece by piece. Molloy's wife stared open-mouthed.

"That's what you and Sister Benignus brought into this house, ma'am," said Molloy bitterly to her. No tears came to Josie's eyes. She hoped they would kill her there and then so that she would not feel it any more, any of it.

"Get your things together now. You're not staying in this house a minute longer, you thieving bitch!"

He spat viciously at her and stormed down the stairs, his wife throwing her a last frightened look as she followed.

In a daze, Josie packed the cardboard suitcase they had given her in the orphanage. She heaped everything she had into it then dressed herself and wandered down the stairs, her limbs weighing her down like iron. Molloy stood in the doorway with his arms folded. He gestured with his thumb. The door closed loudly behind her and Josie stood outside in the first light of dawn. The first birds were starting up in the trees. Josie belted her coat. A country road stretched before her.

Molloy watched her until she was well out of sight.

She spent that night in a haybarn beneath a hessian sack. The following morning she took to the roads again for she wanted to put as much distance as she could between herself and the town. They would all be well familiar by now with Molloy's story, with plenty of his own lies thrown in for good measure. She walked all day without a thought as to her destination or plans for the future. When darkness fell her legs were ready to buckle under her and when the lights of a small cottage appeared at the top of a lane, there was nothing she could do to prevent herself being drawn there. Her stomach was turning over with hunger.

The face that stared out suspiciously from the crack in the door frightened her for a split second but then she saw that it was the face of an old man, listless white strands of hair despairing on a freckled pate. His pupils widened as he looked at her, a young woman come out of nowhere, standing on his doorstep at midnight. He could not take his eyes off her, her clear porcelain face, the slim whitenes of her arms. A tremor ran through him and his voice stumbled in search of words. He pulled his shirt closed and reddened at the thought of his stained vest beneath it. His body began its takeover as he stood there and he was filled with fear but there was nothing he could do to prevent it so he opened the door to admit her. He took the suitcase and left it under the stairs. He felt like he wanted to burst into tears.

Josie drank in her new surroundings, the yellowing holy pictures on the walls, the trousers and braces slung across the back of a chair, the cat sitting on a creel of turf eyeing her jealously. She became aware of the nervous clattering of the cups. It was then she began to realise for the first time that he was more frightened than her. He heaped sugar from a crumpled bag on to a spoon and spilt it on the bare table as he struggled to steer it to his cup.

The sat and drank. Outside the inky clouds lolled. She told him that she had been on her way to the town of Carn, having come from Dublin, but had disembarked in the wrong village and found herself lost in the heart of the countryside. He shaded his eyes with his hand and nodded. Then he cleared away the cups and saucers and rummaged in the cupboard. He took two glasses from the dresser and filled them with whiskey. When she had taken a long draught, Josie's cares became slowly submerged and she did not find it difficult to stare the old man in the eye. His fingers tapped the wet glass. He spoke of his mother and his brother who had both died in the same year. "The worst part of it about here is the lonesomeness," he said. "It can turn your mind. The only one I see week about is Maggie McCaffrey from Lisnaw and half the time she's in her bed. It's no way for a man to live."

He gave himself to the whiskey after that and all the trouble within him poured out in a fever. Until that moment Josie had not known that such weakness was in men as well, she had only seen it before in herself and the girls in the orphanage. As the whiskey dwindled in the bottle, he did not once look at her but gave his life story, paraded it before her and sat slumped in the chair until his speech no longer made sense and his eyes rolled. When she found his head cradled in her lap and her languid hand stroking the dead tendrils of his hair she tried to decipher her confusion and cling to the strength his weakness asked her for. "Please," he slurred, "I never seen a woman like you before. You're so young. I never seen skin like that. I have money. I have anything you want."

He lay crying at the edge of the bed. He looked like a cornered animal. Josie saw now that there was nothing she couldn't do with him. Her youth took his whole strength from him. She felt him shivering as he guided her hand to the buttons of his grey working shirt and she let her fingernails tinkle on the white hairs of his chest. The more she felt his fear, the more assured she became. She removed his clothes as if they were the skin of his body. She eased herself down on him. His limbs twitched. A groan drifted from deep down within him.

Slowly his face became that of Molloy and Culligan, Culligan of the cheery smile. Who leaned over to her in the cinema and whispered, "Put it on." She held the gold pendant in her hand. "I love you," he said. She gripped the old man's hand so tightly that he whimpered like a child and as she saw Culligan's Volkswagen cruising down a country road with him at the wheel sharing one of his bright stories with her, her stomach turned over with bitterness and she stuck her tongue into the back of the old man's throat like a poison dart. He jerked then moaned in pleasure and terror. "Oh you love me Culligan," Josie cried. The whiskey would not let her hold back any of it now and when he began to cry she laughed and laughed. "I never seen a woman before, that's the truth. The only one I ever seen was my sister. Don't laugh at me. Please don't laugh at me!" She raised herself above him as he blubbered into the pillow. Outside a dog howled. For the first time, Josie Keenan felt afraid of nothing. For so long she had hated the proximity of her own sex, their pursed lips and petty vendettas. In the orphanage she had always longed for that moment when she could walk down the avenue, nowhere near her the shadow of the ugly nun with hairs on her chin. She had dreamed there of men who could stroke her with hard, reassuring fingers, who used the word "pretty" to her.

Now she knew how wrong she'd been about it all. Beneath her the old man jerked like a skinned rabbit. Now Josie saw through it all. She saw their cruelty and their pathetic weakness in the face of the power of their own bodies.

There was nothing but disgust in the world, whether it belonged to men or women. She felt as if she had turned to stone as she sat above him in the bed. She stroked his back and he groaned again. "There there," she said, "you poor little thing. Did you never see a girl before?" She spat in Culligan's eye and drove a knife through Molloy's heart as he stood before her with a face like a death mask above the lightbeam of the torch. Then she softened her voice. She could see that he wanted that. It was alien to him, accustomed as he was to his own sweat and the smell of the animals. "Your little Josie is going to be so nice to you, oh so nice. You like that, don't you?"

They lay there inert after that, until the first light of dawn touched the window and his eyes shot open as he reached out into the morning like a drowning man and cried frantically, "Don't leave me! Don't leave me!"

❦

The smell of Josie Keenan began to encroach upon the house. She made one of the bedrooms hers, washed and starched the sheets and placed a flower in a vase on the mantelpiece. When he came home from the fields in the evening, she looked at him with her eyes and that was all he wanted. When she found him in her room staring transfixed at her underclothes, she lifted the petticoat and stroked his cheek with it. "What were you doing in my room, Phil?" she said. "This is a girl's room, you know that. You shouldn't be in a girl's room." She unfolded the garment and spread it on the bed. "What do you want to look at things like that for, Phil? Mm? That's for girls."

When she asked him for money, she told him it was to buy "some nice things for herself" for she knew what this conjured up in his mind, and watched stoically as he rummaged in the bag behind the sink where he kept the money in rolled bundles. "I'm going to buy a nice pair of stockings with that, Phil," she said, and took the bus to a town across the border where she sat on her own in a café listening to a jukebox and eating ice-creams. She knew he would never have the courage to ask what she did with the money. She could take all the dignity he had from him with one flicker of her eyelashes.

He never queried anything she did. The house became hers and he wanted that.

One day, on her return from the town across the border, Josie saw that the door of the house was half-open. Her first instinct was to run but having told herself that it was nothing but another of the irrational fears that had taken root in her since her days in the dark dormitories of the orphanage, she went on and crossed the stile, then walked up the lane to the house. When the door swung open, she saw the white, hair-specked face of Sister Benignus. Beside her, a stocky priest with red jowls stood ominously with his hands behind his back. In the corner, the old man cowered with tears on his cheeks. The silence ticked away. Then the nun cried out in a voice that was creaky with anger, "You have flown in the face of God. You have flung everything back in our faces, you have abused your body which is the temple of the Holy Ghost. You have turned this man away from the path of goodness and virtue. You will have to ask the Lord God for forgiveness. You have become a scarlet woman Josie Keenan. You will have to atone for your sins!" The priest looked away, reddening and sticking a finger inside his stiff white collar. Josie knew it all by heart now, he was just another man, terrified of what his own body might do to him. But she also knew that the nun had no difficulty in staring straight into her eyes and gripping her viciously by the wrist saying, "You are coming with myself and Father Mooney. We are going to take you into the convent. But we will keep a closer eye on you there than we did in the orphanage. This must never get out and cause scandal. You go and get your belongings. You have done enough harm here! You have ruined this poor man's life. He must now pray for his own soul!"

The nun hovered as Josie packed her suitcase. She spotted the petticoat at the bottom of the bed and lifted it, crying, "What is this? What is this? You wore this?" The blood rushed to her forehead and she tore it to pieces like a woman possessed, flinging it to the floor. "We will punish you, it is the only way," she said bitterly.

The priest was waiting for them at the car, stroking his chin anxiously. They drove into Carn by the back roads and approached the convent by the rear entrance. Once more Josie smelt the sickening odour of boiling cabbage wafting to her nostrils. They entered through the kitchens where greasy-haired country girls darted between the bubbling vats. The nun parted company with the priest and when she got Josie on her own, dug her nails into her shoulder and made her fall on her knees beneath the pale bleeding statue in the chapel.

"Tell the blessed virgin, tell the blessed virgin that you repent for the way you have flown in the face of God!" The nails dug in deeper and Josie, knowing well from all the years she had spent in the cold anaemic chapels such as this one, knew what to give her so she began an endless chant of rosary decades and counterfeit whimpers which gave the nun her gratification as she stood with her fat, middle-aged arms folded, conspiring with the chipped statue. "Oh lady most pure," said Josie. "I am heartily sorry for what I've done. I have been a sinner!" But she was a long way now from the stick-limbed girl in a shopcoat who had smiled innocently from behind the counter of Molloy's shop, who had lined up every morning in the freezing corridors of the orphange to have her hair inspected for lice, who had clasped Culligan's pendant lovingly in her palm. She was the woman who saw the brittleness of anything warm and comforting, the cruelty which was provoked by dependence. She gave the nun the performance of helplessness and weakness she craved. Since she had lived with him, her life at last had become her own, none of them could touch her. And now, she could ice over her emotions with ease and feel nothing. She stood outside herself and watched herself snivel and plead at the statue's feet. She felt like laughing. One voice almost travelled downward to the real world crying, "Sister—where did you get the hairs on your chin? You're a lovely-looking woman sister. I'd say Phil Brady would like you to take his thing in your hand when he's finished with your underwear." She held it back however and meekly followed the nun through the echoing corridors to the laundry where she was given a black overall and told to go and change straight away. "You'll not slack here!" snapped the nun. "You'll have no time for your satins here, I can tell you. Oh by the time you're finished here those pretty little hands won't be in any state to flaunt, my girl!"

She stormed off and Josie stared down the corridor after her, thinking of nothing.

The steam of the laundry billowed above the vats as woebegone fifteen-year olds who looked forty pushed baskets on creaking wheels. Josie Keenan, lest she become indolent, was regularly taken to the corridor in the nuns' quarters, kitted out with a new overall, handed a toothbrush and a zinc bucket of soapy water and told to scrub until every single tile was sparkling clean. "Yessister!" replied Josie and set about her task without complaint. The nun lurked in the shadows hoping to apprehend her in a moment of inattention but Josie applied herself and thought of nothing else but her work. In the laundry, the girls quizzed her and spoke in vague, circumspect whispers of babies they had had in outhouses and ditches. Josie told them nothing of her own life. "Don't tell them anything," she repeated silently to herself. "Let nobody know anything."

It was only when its small helpless face came back to her that her inner strength waned. Its eyes kept coming and going when they spoke of these things and one day she found herself crying aloud to one of her workmates, "Stop it! Stop it! I don't want to talk to you!" The young girl looked on in amazement, whitefaced. All she had said was, "There was a girl in here whose baby died on her."

Apart from the one incident, Josie merged anonymously into the workaday life of the laundry and slowly the extra punishments they gave her began to dwindle. She no longer was instructed to scrub toilets with toothbrushes or peel potatoes with scissors. The nun stopped hounding her and turned her attention to other burgeoning recalcitrants.

At night the smell of women washed with kitchen soap turned Josie's stomach.

She left the window of the laundry open on a number of occasions to see if it would be noticed. On each occasion it was still open the following day.

She made her decision to leave the convent six months after the nun had brought her there.

Standing in the corridor, she could still see the blunt outline of the virgin. The black disc of the gong. She held her slippers in her hand and crept to the laundry. She climbed on the wicker basket and eased the window open. The night air wiped the clammy smell of the laundry off her face. It was a short drop to the ground. She was not afraid for she had planned it for so long and she knew every move she was going to make. She put the convent behind her and did not look back until she was far down the avenue. Its twin spires grinned evilly at her. She thought of all those sleeping soft white bodies, all those heaving little breasts. Oh Phil, oh Culligan, wouldn't you all like that? Wouldn't you now?

Phil Brady's face appeared at the window of the cottage, a grotesque mask lit by a candle. He clasped his hand over his mouth in horror. She knew that this time his fear would be greater than his desire, so she opened her blouse and took out one of her breasts for him, slowly kneading it with her fingers. "Please Josie," he said. "You don't know what that priest said to me. You don't know what they can do."

Josie let him speak, then she took his face in her hands and whispered to him, "Oh Phil, I've missed you so much. You were so nice to me."

He crumbled like clay as she stroked his forehead and she said, "I'm going to need some money, Phil."

He looked mournfully at her. "Yes Josie," he said.

At first light she crept to the kitchen and took the stained bag from behind the sink. She put the notes into her slipper and closed the cottage door behind her, setting off for the town across the border. It took her over two hours to walk and her feet were sore and blistered because of the cheap slippers. She bought herself nylon stockings and shoes, as womanly as she could find to rid herself of the clutch of the convent. She treated herself to a large meal in the café with the jukebox. Then she went to the cinema where she spent two calm, soothing hours watching Alan Ladd trudge the black rainy streets of New York in his belted raincoat.

After that, she took a taxi to the docks and waited for the rest of the evening in the terminal until she stepped up the gangway of the Liverpool ferry at ten o'clock that night.

After a week in a boarding house in a dingy back

street not far from the docks, Josie Keenan found herself standing in front of a fat-bellied Englishman with a cloth on his left shoulder who eyed her up and down and said to her, "You'll do, gel. But you gotter remember—the blokes like a nice pretty barmaid. Get yourself a nice dress. I'll pay for it. The blokes what comes into my place—they like a good time. Know what I mean? Doesn't have to be anything serious, mind, but you get my drift." "Yes," replied Josie and thought of the nun tightening her grip on her wrist.

Some days later she found herself pulling the brass pump handles on the counter of the bar in the Bunch of Grapes, bleary-eyed Scotsmen leaning over to touch her. Josie shrugged her shoulders and thrust their drinks at them. The owner put her up in a cosy room with no holy pictures or chipped saints, nothing but a solitary print of Blackpool illuminations adorning the wall.

On her days off, she sauntered through the bustling streets of the city, the town of Carn far behind her. She painted her face and powdered herself. The girl of Molloy's shop and the orphange belonged to another age and when they grabbed at her body or leered at her, it meant nothing to her, she had seen right to the heart of it with the old man.

She wanted no pretence and soon they understood. They did not smooth it over with the respectability of trust and warmth. They pressed five pound notes into her hand and loitered outside the bar after closing time.

She worked in Liverpool for ten years after that and did not leave for Manchester until it transpired that the Bunch of Grapes was to be closed by the brewery. She was given a week's notice and a fortnight's money. She found herself in a pub in Moss Side, following up an advertisement in the city's evening paper. The black faces that stared at her from the shadows did not bother her and the next day she found herself talking across the counter to bright-shirted men from Trinidad and Tobago who rambled at length about tobacco leaves and their children, their eyes falling to her breasts as the alcohol robbed them slowly and steadily of their fragile restraint.

She remained there for six more years, lying on the bed above the pub, listening to the sound of singsong accents as children played on the dilapidated playground in front of the high rise buildings. Then she was told that the pub had been purchased by a supermarket consortium. She was unemployed once more. She went on the hoof again with her adverts ringed in red marker but this time a replacement position did not surface with ease. "We really wanted someone younger," they said.

She searched for over a month without success and then she began to worry. She had saved very little money. She had no home of her own. She could not live forever on the bit she had put away. One day, after a particularly fruitless day's searching, she was amazed to find herself crying. "There's nothing here for me now," she said to herself but fought off the dark feeling of helplessness that was moving in on her. As she lay in bed that night, she thought of Carn over and over again. She thought of Phil Brady, his face muscles jerking as he heaved above her. She went to the mirror and examined herself. "I've got to live somehow," she said to herself. "In Carn the old men would have nobody. The nuns and priests have seen to that. I don't care about them now. They've had their day with me. I'm no sixteen-year old child now. Let them try to tackle me now."

The following day she went to a department store and bought herself a selection of satin underwear. She laid it on the bed then tried it on. She examined her skin again, for blemishes.

"There's nothing else for me to do," she said.

The following day she went down to the booking office in Deansgate and bought herself a one-way ticket to Ireland.

❧

And now she found herself standing in the lounge bar of the Railway Hotel trying to make sense of what she saw before her. Middle-aged women argued over the most appropriate dressing for a salad niçoise as their well-nourished children cavorted brashly. Above the entrance, flags fluttered gaily and announcements crackled from loudspeakers in the main street. Long lines of parked cars stretched for a mile outside the town.

It seemed as if the town of Carn, the town in which she had been born and reared, a huddled clump of windswept grey buildings split in two by a muddied main street, had somehow been spirited away and supplanted by a thriving, bustling place which bore no resemblance whatever to it.

She left the hotel and walked to The Diamond where a young girl in dancing costume tightened her thin body and kicked her legs high in the air as a row of adjudicators on the makeshift stage consulted their clipboards judiciously. Many of the old shopfronts had been replaced. Any that she remembered had been completely repainted and refurbished. Josie could not believe her eyes when she found herself standing outside the pub where her father, the Buyer Keenan, had spent many of his waking hours. Once called the Greyhound Bàr, now a neon sign spread in an arc above the door read the TURNPIKE INN. A poster advertised *Crazy Crazy Nites*.

When she came to the graveyard she felt the pain growing inside her again as she stared at the gravestones of her father and mother.

Michael Joseph Keenan, R.I.P.
Kathleen Josephine Keenan 1898–1946 R.I.P.

For a split second she saw her own death, a gunmetal face fixed on the sky, all around the faces and voices of Carn as she had known it. The graveyard overlooked the town. Below her, she could see the crowds streaming from the dancehall, The Sapphire Ballroom.

The fields about her were specked with forget-me-nots and a long-forgotten day came into her mind, her mother with a basket bending down to pick them in the same fields, Josie by her side in white socks and a pink check dress.

Josie Keenan had come home to the town of Carn, the only home she knew.

V

"Are you going to lie there all day? Do you think I have nothing better to do than run up and down after you—is that it?

Sadie Rooney's mother shut the door loudly behind her and with that the Aston Martin in which Sadie and her companion Steve McQueen had been splicing the wind together, dissipated like smoke and Sadie's eyes travelled the red flock wallpaper before coming to rest on the weary face of the Infant of Prague on the mantelpiece. She shook her head and moistened the dry roof of her mouth with her tongue, then tumbled onto the floor and stood at the window scratching her arm as she waited for some sort of order to come into her mind.

Outside the town was cranking into life. Indeed, thought Sadie, life is right.

The words of the butcher came to her. "Do you know," he said, "this is the best wee town in Ireland. I mean, you have everything you want here. You have a picture house. And the dances. You couldn't meet friendlier people. And what about the celebrations last year for Matt Dolan? No other town has anything like that! The bands and the parades!"

Carn, thought Sadie, Carn, Carn, Carn. Nowhere but Carn. Carn—the beginning and the end. Nothing else in the whole wide world but it and its cramped streets.

She could see it all unwinding from her bedroom. Jacko the grocer taking out his cabbage crates whistling. Mrs Wilson screwing up her nose. "Are them cabbage fresh?" She looked at him as if she suspected him of injecting them with a deadly poison. "Fresh? Fresh, Mrs? Did you ever know me to sell bad cabbage? There you are." He heaped two fat-headed cabbages into her arms and off she went, beaming. Then along came Grouse Monaghan and urinated on a lampost. In the doorway of the supermarket, Mrs Reilly and Mrs McKenna swopped domestic tales. Sadie knew their style. "I have awful trouble with Declan and this constipation. He was on the pot for nearly a whole hour last night, nearly a whole hour I waited—and do you know what I got for my trouble?"

"No—what?"

"Wee hard balls."

Then they stood looking at each other as if they had just overheard the announcement of world war three.

As Sadie pulled on her dress, she caught a glimpse of a bin on two wheels coming around the corner. It was Blast Morgan—who else could it be?

Regular as clockwork, the cap parked askew on his head and half an inch of ash dangling from his lips as he made his way through the morning blinking at the light. He took off the cap and leaned against a wall to relight his cigarette. *Blast this, blast that, blast that cold, blast that heat*. Then he donned his cap once more and set off again. After that they all did their turn, the minute hand of a clock pressing predictably onward. Sadie knew them, every one, their time and their place, where they were coming from and where they were going to.

At the top of his garden, just beneath the window, Mr Galvin began his day's work with the snip of a garden shears.

The meat plant horn hooted.

Lawn mowers began to whirr.

Carpets were beaten in the lane.

The churchbell went ding dong four times an hour.

The chickenhouse fan hummed.

On it goes, thought Sadie, on and on and on.

The tick tock days of Carn, a market town half a mile from the border.

She clipped on an earring and said to herself in the wardrobe mirror, "Wotcher, gel! Going down the Old Kent Road, then?"

Through the markets of Portobello she sauntered and then home to the flat in Walm Lane Willesden, armed to the teeth with trinkets.

"That's wot I want, innit?" she said to The Infant Of Prague. "Oh, Carn's okay; but I 'aven't started living yet, 'ave I? Do you get my drift, Infant Of Prague?"

She sat on the edge of the bed and wiggled her toes. Sandie Shaw Sadie. Mr Galvin came into her head. "You're all the modern girl," he smiled, "that's what you are young Rooney. All mad for the pop orchestras and the short skirts. What would the likes of us around here know about the like of that? We went out with the ark."

Sadie shook her head. "Well one way or another, I'm getting out Mr Galvin. I'm not staying here to spend my life waiting for Blast to come around the corner every morning."

"I don't blame you one little bit," he replied, "that Blast would drive anybody out."

Sadie tidied up her room and went downstairs where her mother put her breakfast brusquely in front of her villifying a guitar-playing priest she had heard talking about teenage parties on the radio the night before.

"That's what we've come to expect," she said acidly. "But not in this house, I can tell you."

Sadie finished up her breakfast and set off for the packing shed of Carn Poultry Products where she was due to begin work at two.

"They're coming today."

Una Lacey put down the phone. "We'll have some action now Sadie," she said.

So they were coming. All the way from London. There were two girls. Carol and Jane. And a boy. A fella. A bloke. All Una's cousins. From redbus London, with tales by the score of mods and rockers and with-it princes in clubs and discoes that stayed open the whole night long. Sadie could not wait.

They both lay on the fairgreen looking up at the blue glass of the sky. "You just want to see their clothes," said Una. "They have everything they want. They get far more money that we ever see. But they're good crack. At least the girls are. I don't know what he's like."

Sadie tried to imagine what he looked like. She thought of a thousand faces but could not choose any single one. "What does he work at?" she asked Una.

"He doesn't work. He goes to art college."

Art College. John Lennon had been to one. They lived a wild life in those places. There were girls there. Girls who were not afraid to speak their mind and live whatever way they wanted. He would be well used to girls.

So that's that, she said to herself resignedly.

They lay there until it was time to go and meet them. Sadie's spine tingled as they watched the vehicles from the distant towns and the more remote hamlets of the hinterland unload.

Then Una stood on her tiptoes and waved. When Sadie saw them appear, she instantly felt as if she were dressed in rags. She wanted to rush into the public toilet and bar the door. They wore pearls and their slim wrists jangled with bracelets. Their lipstick was bright pink, their faces made up to the nines. Their London accents seemed to soar high above the rooftops and sit in the clouds like magic. Their perfume filled the air. A farmer on his way home stopped dead in the middle of the The Diamond and stood staring with his mouth open as if he were hallucinating. They set down their suitcases and lit cigarettes. "Oh girls—this is my pal Sadie." They smiled broadly and shook hands. Then Sadie heard another voice, a male London voice. He had hair like George Harrison, a moptop cut above the ears. He wore a brown corduroy waistcoat and a striped shirt. She followed his bright hipster trousers all the way down to his elasticated suede boots. She was so overwhelmed she didn't know what to say and was glad of the distraction when Una thrust a case into her hand.

They set off down the road together, alive with chatter, and when Sadie Rooney set off for home, she felt as though she were cruising six inches above the road.

Through the open door of the Golden Chip Bob Dylan shouted that he'd got no secrets to conceal, the girls from The Park draped across the shimmering chrome of the jukebox as if they were trying to climb inside his very words.

Sadie tensed as she saw them come in. He was with them. "There you are Sadie," called Una. "Here Dave, you sit down there beside Sadie."

He smiled and sat beside her. She reddened. They ordered coffees and after that the conversation wandered to where she had hoped it would, to the beaches of Brighton where a phalanx of motorcycles stood outside a hotel, leather-jacketed rockers fondling chains as they faced the oncoming mods in their knee-length parkas. "I love the Beatles," he said. "I've got all their albums."

Albums he calls them, thought Sadie. Not records. Or long players. Or elpees. Albums.

"Those rockers, they would really do for you," said Carol, tapping ash into the tray.

"What's this about you being in a group?" Una said cheekily to him. "Are you?"

He nodded. "The Trygons. We play The Stones. And The Who. And our own songs."

"They're fab," said Carol.

Afterwards they set off for the carnival dance, linking each other, smoking cigarettes and singing. Reared in the teeming surburbs of London, they had more to worry them than sour old men and crotchetty women so for their benefit they wiggled their hips and sang even louder. Dave walked on ahead, trying to make sense of his new surroundings, the tiny shops and littered streets. Down at the carnival, mock screams carried upward into the navy blue sky, sparks from the dodgems fantailed above the cacophony. Frank Sinatra crooned from a hanging loudspeaker, his intimacy wrapping its arms around the town. The swingboats seemed to stop just short of the moon. They tossed pennies on to chequerboards, Dave picking out a bullseye on a target with one single shot.

The dancers made their way in scattered knots to a marquee decked with coloured lights. "Dancing in a tent?" Dave cried incredulously.

Inside, oil-slicked countrymen clustered together beside the mineral crates, hiding behind the smoke and stealing mouthfuls from hidden whiskey bottles. Girls fawned adoringly over the band. The singer kicked his instep and winked, pasting back his accordeon-pleated hair. Dave and the girls stared in wonder as if they had come upon a secret commune of Martians. They stared at the six poles supporting the canvas. They stared at the band's blazers.. They stared at the posters advertising treasure hunts and parish socials. They had tumbled back in time, lost in space at the Carn annual grand carnival. The locals eyed them viciously as they danced, narrowed their eyes and stood with their arms folded. When Dave went down on this hunkers to do the Woolly Bully with Carol, they muttered under their breath, "Woolly bully—Woolly Fucky!"

Carried along on the tidal wave of their confidence, Sadie came into her own. She danced for all she was worth, the canvas became the sky over London.

Dave clicked his fingers and mouthed the words of the songs. They danced until the band stood upright with chins out and announced the national anthem. The jealous countrymen at the back hoped that Dave would give them an excuse to put an end to his cockiness but he didn't, he stood like the rest and then they walked home, past the padlocked amusements and Sadie Rooney went rigid when she felt an arm slowly circle about her waist and heard his soft voice say, "Can I walk home with you?"

Sadie looked at the stars above the town and kissed

his lips as he said, "See you tomorrow then Sadie, okay?"

She wanted to say tell me more about the band about the tubes about Trafalgar Square about Soho please tell me but she couldn't. She just looked at him and played with a shirt button, then watched him walk down the lane and went inside to face her mother.

But when she started into her tirade, for the first time Sadie heard none of it, it was as if she were floating in the vastness of a black sky, adrift like a spaceman from his craft and away from all that was grey in the town of Carn. Somehow a gap had opened and as her mother ranted, Sadie clutched at the new warmth she was feeling for all she was worth, the words "insolent" and "discipline" tiny irrelevant lights that winked somewhere miles below her on the earth.

They spent all their time together after that. Carol and Jane fluttered their eyelashes when they appeared, cooing, "'Ere's the two lovebirds. Where 'ave you been then?"

Una Lacey took Sadie aside and whispered, "You know what Sadie? They're all mad jealous in the factory. They say you've turned into a snob, that you won't talk to them. What do you care about them Sadie?"

Sadie shrugged her shoulders and smiled for she knew that she wouldn't have to put up with the small, envious minds of Carn for much longer. As she lay on the fairgreen watching Dave Robinson from Islington fashion daisy chains, she silently embroidered their phrases into her own speech. "Clever clogs," she said to herself, and "Innit?"

In her mind she was a long way from the fair-green.

And soon she would be further. The strobelights of the The River Club melting on her face. They lay by the lake and boys Sadie knew sidled up to Carol and Jane insisting, "I can swim out to the island. I can. Would you like me to show you?" They almost cried with frustration when they saw Dave lock his thumbs into the buckle of his hipsters. Such effortlessness was far beyond them.

"This is ace," said Dave, "really ace."

When the first stories reached her ears in the factory canteen, Sadie knew their jealously had got the better of them. They leaned over clandestinely to each other and threw mysterious expressions in her direction. They raised their voices slightly when they mentioned his name. At first Sadie paid no attention, well aware that any reaction on her part would only whet their appetites. They folded their arms on their chests and nodded knowingly. They talked behind cupped hands. When Sadie appeared they broke into excited laughter and then went back to their tasks suddenly.

Resentment began to grow in Sadie. It gnawed at her all day long much as she tried to submerge it. She knew why they were jealous of her. They were jealous because she would not let herself be stuck in Carn for the rest of her life. They did not want to be shown up so they were turning on her.

"They're bitches," she said to Una when the canteen had closed one Friday afternoon. "Imagine making up all those stories. How could they stoop so low?"

Una said nothing, picked at her nail and looked away emptily.

"Do you know what I heard one of them saying in the freezer when she knew I was coming? Why would he bother with the likes of her when he has Surgeon McDonagh's daughter from Trinity College chasing him around the town? They're jealous bitches so they are. Aren't they Una?"

Una shrugged her shoulders but did not reply.

"They didn't have to say that," Sadie went on. "That's an awful thing to say. I don't care how jealous they are."

Una lit a cigarette. She blew out the match and stared at the dead black head for a moment, then said, "It's true Sadie."

Sadie felt as if the canteen had suddenly tilted on its side. "What?" she said, her voice trembling. Una dragged on the cigarette and bit her lip. "He was with her after you left him on Friday night."

Sadie's mouth dried up. The smoke seemed to swirl all about her. She felt the redness coming to her face. She awkwardly gathered up the delf and cutlery and tried to smile but she knew Una could see right into her mind and it froze.

She went back to the factory floor feeling cold but with her face burning. Every exchange between her workmates, no matter how innocent made her want to be sick. She felt as if she had a vile skin disease she had brought upon herself.

When she was collecting her pay packet in the office that evening, a group of girls behind her purposely knocked against her and said, "Look who's in front of us—Lady Muck from London. I wonder where she's bringing Mr Stuck-up tonight?"

She pushed past them and when she was safely out of sight, she ran from their taunts and when she got home, she swore to herself that it wasn't true, that somehow Una had got it wrong but she still couldn't stop the tears, and when she waited for him on The Diamond that evening she felt as if the whole town was preparing itself for her meeting with Dave Robinson.

✿

A small rowing boat bobbed as Dave stared across the blue mirror of the lake in silence. Sadie tried to steady her voice. "I've made a fool of myself. You've made a show of me in front of everyone."

He did not reply for a long time, then suddenly he turned and said sharply, "I don't have to listen to you going on like this Sadie. For Christ's sake, we're not married or anything. I only took a girl out a couple of times. Nothing more."

A fishing reel spun in the distance. Sadie tried to gather her thoughts. All the pictures she had built up in her mind since meeting him now winged away liked birds.

"You take life too seriously anyway Sadie. It's just a holiday. It's just a bit of fun."

He held her by the arms and kissed her on the forehead but she did not feel it for her flesh was like marble and when they walked back to town, she left him when they came to The Diamond for she could not bear the thought of the eyes peering from the twitching curtains and the shadows of the shop doorways. He squeezed her hand and said goodbye. "Maybe someday you can come over and hear the Trygons," he laughed. Sadie just stared blankly after him then turned and walked down the main street, the shadows of the hot summer day all around her.

The first week after that was the hardest. She was hit on the neck by a flying gizzard and did not turn around when she heard one of them say, "He was with a different one on Saturday night. Talk about being led up the garden path. She'll be damn glad of us yet."

Una Lacey consoled her on the way home. "What do you care about him Sadie? There's plenty more fish in the sea. A fellow with a car, that's what we want."

Sadie nodded but it meant nothing to her. When Una asked her if she would be going to the Golden Chip that night, she just shook her head. She felt that none of it was worth fighting any more.

She would just drift with it and it could take her wherever it would.

Her mother was the first to remark on the change

in Sadie after that. She said to her neighbours, "I think Sadie is getting a bit of sense at last. She's a great help to me about the house these days." In the factory too, the change was evident. She did not now turn away when they spoke about a local boy who would be "a good catch". Nor when they effusively described house interiors or baby clothes. She became afraid that any lack of interest on her part might prompt a return to the animosity they had harboured towards her in the past. When she visited the boutique, she no longer automatically chose the brightest clothes but selected something she felt would attract less attention and closer to their taste. The English inflections in her speech disappeared. She dated boys from the factories and listened attentively as they spoke at length about motor car engines and farm work. When a glittering new engagement ring was proffered in the canteen, Sadie beamed with the rest in order that she might be drawn closer to them, eager for the protection and security of mundanity. She dreaded a return to the probing eyes and the whispers of "Look who's come down in the world then", to the sweat on her palms and the redness of her face.

When it was announced that one of them was "tying the knot", they all cheered and Sadie said nothing at all about the empty feeling inside her.

And when she went home and the blackest of moods took her over, there was nothing she wanted to say, to anyone.

When the first notices advertising *Purple Pussycat—Ireland's wildest rock group!* were put up in The Sapphire Ballroom, Sadie Rooney paid them no attention. She had heard them speak derisively of it at work but it was of no consequence to her, until one evening on her way home from the factory Sadie was startled out of her daydream by a loud Dublin voice and looked up to find herself confronted by the headbanded figure of a six foot male and his female companion in a long print skirt. They smiled out at her from an assemblage of pots and pans roped to an orange haversack.

"We're looking for some place to camp," they said. "We're here for the Purple Pussycat gig. We've hitched from the city."

Sadie directed them to the Hairy Mountains and stared after them, a nervous excitement growing in her stomach. She could not sleep that night and no one was more surprised than Una Lacey when Sadie arrived at the Golden Chip that following night. "Are you going to The Sapphire Sadie?" asked Una. "I thought you'd given all that up."

"Oh I just thought I'd go and have a look," Sadie replied.

"They're a right-looking shower. There's a gang of them camped out at the Hairy Mountains. A rare looking bunch of madmen if you ask me."

The band was already on stage when they got to The Sapphire. Goosepimples crawled on Sadie's back as she watched the singer fall to his knees clutching the microphone like a chalice, the circling glitterball tossing specks of light on his t-shirt. A howl curled from the swaying mane of beard, *Baby I neeeeeeed you sooooooo baaaaaaaaaaaad!* The jiving girls stood back, perplexed and not far from anger. The drums sent out a throbbing rhythm as the singer, still on his knees, spoke of love and harmony. "How are you tonight, Carn? Are you feeling all right?"

The dancers stood motionless in the centre of the hall. They were dumbfounded. "What's going on?" they said. "That isn't singing." Eventually they cobbled together whatever rhythm they could and continued around the floor in a half-daze.

Sadie was in a daze herself, almost swooning under the relentless onslaught of male bodies that surged forward at the beginning of each dance. She looked up to see an outstretched arm and a long-haired youth at the end of it saying, "Dance?"

He told her he was from Dublin and was with the people camping in the Hairy Mountains. They were setting off travelling the following day, he said. This was going to be their last night in Ireland for a very long time.

"Where are you going?" Sadie asked anxiously.

She knew he was going to London. She just knew.

"Europe," he said. "First Amsterdam—then who knows?"

His eyes were half-closed as he rolled a cigarette. "There's five of us. We have no problem making out. We make things."

He dragged on the cigarette and smiled. He put his arm around her shoulder. The singer lay on his back and howled again.

Cars revved up and sped off into the night. Stray couples courted at the back of the dancehall. A fight threatened and bodies thrust themselves forward. Voices rose and dipped again, the gathering breaking up raggedly. Sadie Rooney, her back against the pebbledashed wall of the ballroom, stared up at the denim clad youth who said his name was Danny. He tickled her on the chin and smiled again. "All you need is thirty quid and you're in," he said. "Six is a perfect number." Then he reached in his pocket and said, "I have something for you." It was a tiny rabbit's foot on a leather thong. "I want you to have it. Even if you don't come, I want you to have it." She clutched it in her hand and he kissed her.

They stood outside the Railway Hotel. "We're leaving at ten from here, this very spot. Promise me you'll be here."

"Yes," Sadie said.

He nodded and then went off towards the Hairy Mountains. Sadie was unsteady with nervousness on her way home. She could not keep her hand from trembling as she spooned the tea into the pot. The late night deejay played a special request for all the young lovers of the world. At once Sadie found herself retreating to the security of the factory voices and rushing in fear away from them. Her head was a mass of jumbled wires. The side of her face was numb and her palms were drenched in sweat. The kitchen door opened. Her mother stood there in her dressing gown.

"I didn't know you were going to be late."

Sadie stammered awkwardly. "Please ma," she began. "There's something I want to ask you."

Her mother looked quizzically at her and replied, "Hadn't you the whole day to ask me? A fine time to pick to ask anything when the rest of the Christian world are asleep in their beds. Go on up to bed before you have him down."

She closed the door behind her and Sadie just stood in the middle of the kitchen. A lightness came into her head. She put away the dishes and the teapot. Then she switched off the radio and went upstairs.

She lay there beneath the ceiling and felt as if every drop of blood had been drained from her body. She could not stop her heart from racing.

She lay there until first light. Outside she heard the sound of the first footsteps making their way down the lane to work.

As the sun rose above Railway Terrace, she stared out towards the blunt silhouettes of the Hairy Mountains and saw in her mind the purring van waiting by the Railway Hotel, Danny anxiously checking his watch, then the sliding door being pulled shut, and as the engine revved up and turned towards the Dublin Road, Sadie began to weep as she cried silently and bitterly to herself, "I hate you Sadie Rooney, I hate you, I hate you, I fucking hate you!"

VI

Time passed and Carn got into its stride.

The hottest summer for years came to the town. Through the open windows of the terraces wafted the smell of atrophying innards, along with the sound of tapping hammers but not a soul complained for it was James Cooney's message that business was booming, and as the new extension of the Carn Meat Plant inched its way along the hill overlooking the town, the housewives and children went contentedly about their daily tasks, secure in the knowledge that all was well. And getting better. For, on the day the final rivet went in, the Turnpike Inn hummed with the news that forty new workers were wanted on the spot by James Cooney. And so Benny Dolan, along with his schoolmate Joe Noonan, found himself in the head office being surveyed up and down. The foreman wiped bloodstained fingers on his apron and said, "You're Dolan. Your father and me went to school together. A wild man in his day, eh? I'm only codding you son. Do you see that woman below in the yard? you'll be working on the line with her.

Maisie Lynch is her name. Half daft but there's no harm in her. Divides her time between here and the mental. If you have any trouble, see me."

He threw them overalls and caps.

Maisie Lynch stood back with her hands on her hips and rasped at them, "Youse needn't think youse'll slack here! I'm in charge! Do youse hear that?"

"Right Maisie," said Benny.

In the afternoons, the streets buzzed. The jukebox played in the Golden Chip, workers horseplayed throwing salt and sugar across the tables. The Turnpike Inn began to sell coffee and steak and kidney pies. Benny and Joe became friendly with the older workers, throwing darts and playing cards. They went drinking with them every Friday after work, stayed until closing time and emerged swaying and singing. "Good man young Dolan, you're a good one. Your father was out there when the real fighting was going on!" They sang rebel songs all the way home, cursing England and British Imperialism much to the amusement of the smiling sergeant who was taking up his position outside the barracks to observe the patrons on their way to The Sapphire. Across town another voice echoed, "Fair play to James Cooney and to hell with the railway. What good is a Mickey Mouse railway to anyone? Carn's flying now and nobody can say different. Here we go, boys, and let anyone stand in our way. Fifty quid of a bonus this week and I don't care who hears it!"

When Benny arrived into work complaining of a hangover like the rest of them, Maisie Lynch twisted up her face and said, "If you'd do your work, it would be more in your line. Do you think I'm going to pack all these by myself just because you've spent your night pissing your money up against Cooney's wall? Well you've another think coming. You young people have it too easy, that's what's wrong. When I was your age, do you know what I had? I hadn't even shoes on my feet. You don't know what hardship is! Pack them hearts and less buck out of you!"

"That's the stuff, Maisie," called someone from the yard, "you tell them. The smell of a barman's apron'd knock them."

"I say Maisie," called another voice, "would you take it?"

Maisie screwed up her face. "Take it? Take what?"

"Six inches. Thick!"

Maisie flung her cap on the floor and disappeared into the toilet, muttering to herself.

"Jesus," said Joe Noonan, "what a spot."

By the end of his first month Benny felt as if he'd been in the factory for years. The summer stretched before him. He felt there was nothing he couldn't do.

When the new motorcycle shop opened, he spent his evenings after work admiring the machines, chatting with the young mechanic who had moved from the north to avail himself of the new prosperity. They discussed brand names and maintenance at length. In the end Benny settled for a Yamaha 750 c.c. and took it for its maiden run all the way to Bundoran in Donegal. Joe Noonan cheered as they roared up the main street watched by gawping children and sullen adolescents. They bought a six-pack of beer and lay on the strand with straw hats over their eyes. "Hey amigo, she some machine, no?" said Joe with a broad grin.

"Si senor," answered Benny, "she cost me mucho dollar."

❦

The local football stadium, for years choked with weeds and scored with graffiti, now, thanks to a donation from James Cooney who had recently become the club sponsor, sat proudly in all its refurbished splendour at the top of the town. This new-found interest in the club seemed to fire the players with a new dynamism. After years of abject failure and poor attendances, the mightiest teams in the province suddenly began to fall before them. Each week the Pride Of Carn Marching Band circled the returfed pitch proudly before the match. The supporters followed their heroes to all corners of the country, carousing until all hours in distant towns. Una Lacey's father, Pat, the club's newly-elected president, took most of the credit for the team's success. From the moment he had taken over, all troubles that had for so long seemed to dog the team, melted into thin air. Pat Lacey had the Midas touch when it came to management and organisation of the team—there was no one in Carn who would argue with that.

"There is nothing that Carn Rovers cannot do," he

cried after yet another victory as he waved to the jubilant crowds on the terraces. "We are going to conquer all before us."

From the window of the photographer's shop, the ever-growing pyramid of trophies reflected their boundless pride back at the people. The team became known as Lacey's Lions. And wherever the flag-decked coaches went, Joe and Benny followed on their decorated bikes chanting, "Rovers Rovers" as they roared through the wideyed villages of the midlands.

Every week, as his victorious team made their way to the dressing room, Pat Lacey was joined by Father Kelly and James Cooney and, as the cheers rose to the sky, the people felt indissolubly bonded together by their faith in these men who now could no wrong.

One warm Saturday in early July, Benny and Joe set off at the crack of dawn to watch their team ride over Drogheda United like a mighty wave. They stood in the market square whirling scarves as the dejected supporters of the vanquished team slunk home through the dusty streets.

By the time they got back to Carn, the weekend festivities were in full swing and they shouted, "Hey you guys—look out! Carn's Hell's Angels are back in town!"

They parked the bike outside the Turnpike and went inside where a group of women were cheering as one of their number, a mature red-cheeked woman, bumped and grinded on a table, pulling her dress coquettishly above her knee. They clapped along frenziedly as Joe said to the barman, "We hope you

no gringo senor. You know what we do weet gringo?
We keel heem."

"Two pints," interrupted Benny, "and less lip
Cisco."

At the end of July a notice appeared on the telegraph
pole outside the meat plant and subsequently was to
be seen covering every wall in the town. It read:

> All-Ireland Fleadh Cheoil
> Festival of Music for Young and Old!
> All roads lead to Carn August 1967!

Beneath the circus-red typeface a stick man cavorted
and played a tin whistle. Benny and Joe tucked their
biscuit tins under their arms and said, "Now we'll see
some real action!"

They squeezed the bulging hearts into their tight
plastic containers as Maisie ranted furiously to
herself about this latest development.

"If the priest had any say left, there'd be no festival
in this town! There'll be no licentious behaviour in
the town of Carn. Don't think I don't know what goes
on. And you—you and your big motorbike, or who
do you think you are? I see what goes on all right. I see
them with their gins and tonics lying with their legs
open for all the tramps of the day. Twenty years ago I
know what they'd have got. But now? Into the bin

with the holy pictures and bare your arse for the whole country. They'll rue the day they let the whoremasters into this town, festival or no festival!"

A marquee was erected on the fairgreen. Primary school teachers loaded down with violin cases and brochures bustled through the town all day long. Bunting was draped across the main street. Hotel yards were converted into public bars, with crude painted wooden notices advertising *sangwitches* and *minerals*.

Tents appeared in odd places, long-haired youths in Aran sweaters loitered outside the hotel drinking out of paper cups. Bikers roared in on massive machines and converged on The Diamond. Benny and Joe drank with them into the small hours, listened eagerly as they swopped stories of Californian Highways and European autobahns. They came from Waterford and the north but there was nowhere they hadn't been. Chains dangled from their leather jackets, they wore studded wristlets. The longhairs joined them and tuned up a guitar. From behind a swaying mane of hair a melody went up and the bikers sang along with their glasses raised. Joe Noonan took the instrument and sang a number by Donovan Leitch the Scottish minstrel. Then they went back to their tents and sang until dawn, stumbling back into town in time for the opening of one of the makeshift bars.

"This sure is some machine you have, man," said one of the bikers to Benny. "You guys sure know what you're at. If you're ever in Waterford, make sure and give us a call."

Beer-bellied ballad singers thrust out their stomachs and sang songs about Mexican peasants and Irish emigrants with equal enthusiasm. A crackling public address system struggled to be heard as it announced details of forthcoming competitions. Francie Mohan stood in the centre of The Diamond and waved a bottle as he cried, "Hah! You never thought you'd live to see the like of this, did youse? We're a long way now from the boat train and the brown paper parcel! Here we go, the sky's the limit, all we need now is Ulster back!"

All along the roads leading into the town, prone bodies lay scattered beside empty crates and bottles. The longhairs seemed to be everywhere. They washed their clothes in the fountain and romped naked in the lake. An unsavoury incident had provoked a near-riot at a meeting of the urban council. A pair of men's underpants had been draped over the Matt Dolan Memorial Plaque. "The men of 1916 didn't die for these unwashed bastards!" the chairman snapped.

But the shopkeepers didn't concur as their tills were ringing like never before, so there was little more about it. Even when a youth climbed on the roof of the library and stood there in his pelt singing, *"Even the president of the United States one day has to stand naked"* the shopkeepers would not relent. They said that it was police business and no concern of theirs. They were there to trade and nothing more. Through the open window of the cinema, loud rock music blared, the soundtrack of the film which was showing, carefully selected by the projectonist for this week, *The Sweet Ride.*

The bikers and the longhairs sat back with their arms folded and their legs up on the seats and watched with glee as their American counterparts zoomed across the sand on mighty motorbikes and threatened to reduce roadside cafés to rubble unless they were supplied with the day's takings. They cheered from the front row where they sat munching crisps and drinking lager as the fuzz-bearded angel flung the puny owner right across his own shop. By the time the film drew to a close, the atmosphere in the cinema had risen to a frenzied climax, and the bikers climbed on each others' backs as a girl in a wet t-shirt wiggled her breasts provocatively.

The film became the talk of the town.

The priest was apopleptic in the pulpit.

The Fleadh Cheoil went on for three days. The streets were littered with battered cartons and beer cans. The bunting drooped forlornly over the main street. A smashed plate glass window looked emptily out from the draper's premises. The barmen began to take down their wooden signs and sweep up the yards. Benny and Joe gave the bikers a firm handclasp.

"Come back to Carn," they said. "It was real good to meet you."

"Carn Bikers Okay," said the Waterford Angels.

Joe and Benny stood watching them leave, followed by the dilapidated caravan of the longhairs with their pots and pans, waving to them as they faded from sight.

"My head is lifting off me," said Joe, "three days on the trot."

Benny hopped on the Yamaha and shook his head,

then off they went to have a last one for their Waterford brothers.

The following week the priest could not contain his fury. He was so upset that at times it looked as if he was about to use a few expletives himself. "What would our forefathers have thought?" he asked wistfully. He went on to say that people had now too much money. Too much of everything. They were like tigers who having once tasted blood, were now mad for more. More of everything. The parishioners looked at each other, redfaced. He quoted statistics from other European countries and alluded to life-styles propogated by the glossy magazines and the seamier English dailies. "We are on a slippery slope," he concluded darkly.

The congregation gathered in small groups outside in the churchyard, smoking cigarettes and fiddling nervously with their prayerbooks. They said that the priest was right, that people in the old days, in the days of the railway and before that even were better off. "Do we want the place to be like Hollywood?" said an elderly man. But then the conversation turned to other topics and by the time they got home, they had forgotten everything the priest had said for it could not stand up to the seduction of an afternoon's television and the smell of cooking roast beef.

Benny and Joe spent very few weekends in Carn after that. Joe had bought himself a Suzuki and together they found themselves in the cities and larger towns of the north. Wherever their favourite bands were to be found, they made their way there, standing at the back of the dancehall with their helmets in hand, until they eventually left with local girls who prodded them with questions about their bikes and where they came from. "We're the Carn Angels," said Benny with a smile. "Eh Joe?"

"Si senor—whatever you do, don't mess with ze Carn Angels."

They sat with the girls outside their tent as Joe strummed a tune. "You're great on the guitar," they said, "there's no fellas around here like you boys. Where are you going next? Can we come?"

In the city of Dublin they sauntered through the shops that had begun to spring up around the Dandelion market and the girls moved closer to them as they priced bottles of patchouli and Indian pipes, the longhairs passing them across the counter with the misty-eyed nod of understanding that had of late become an international semaphore. They went to parties in the city's flatland where the air was thick with the smell of Lebanese Red dope and the sound of Pink Floyd meandered until dawn. They sat in cafés and drank endless cups of coffee.

"I wonder what Maisie would do with an auld joint, eh?" laughed Benny.

When they found themselves on the highways of Europe, it seemed that Carn was a distant place that belonged only in the dim recesses of memory. They sat in Dam Square and watched the pigeons fluttering into the sky like leaves as moustachioed policemen strolled casually past them.

Joe drummed on his helmet and said, "Beats Belturbet of a Friday night anyhow."

They cruised as far as Istanbul and then the money ran out.

"I told you youse'd come to a bad end," mocked Joe in his Maisie Lynch voice. "Youse had no business running to them places. You could get a class of a disease out yonder."

They spent their last night in a camp outside Paris. The moon rose up above them and foreign voices clacked in the nearby tents as Benny lay back on the bank of the river and slugged the last of the cider. He turned to Joe who was lying beside him and as the flagon spun into the sky above him, Benny said, "Are you all right there Joe boy?"

"Never was better senor."

And when they hit home three days later the birds were getting ready in the trees and on the wires and Blast Morgan was just beginning his tour of the gutters and pavements of main street. They grinned sleepily as they saw yet another trophy had climbed to the top of the pyramid in the photographer's window, and high up on the hill the first lights were coming on in James Cooney's new extension which had just received news of a massive order from Saudi Arabia.

VII

The Sacred Heart of Jesus looked down on Josie
Keenan and outside the wind blew across the Hairy
Mountains. Affixed to the oleograph, a small red
lamp sent its shadows about the room. "I'd appreciate
you leaving it there, we were reared with it like," the
farmer had said when giving her the key. The flowing
golden locks fell on Christ's shoulders and he pitied
her. Once upon a time those same eyes had spent their
days overseeing the daily life of God-fearing decent
people, who toiled and trudged long hours in the
fields and returned only at night to be fortified by
griddle cake and buttermilk before falling on their
knees to give thanks for their little bit of ground and
the strength in their limbs. Eyes that kept a constant
vigil in a town that had yet to know even the
prosperity of the railway never mind meat plants,
ruled then with an iron fist by a red-faced bull of a
clergyman who rode his mare with his riding crop in
hand, who could by his own admission perform
miracles. Cassie, Josie's mother had known that town
in her youth and had heard at first hand the story of

the miracle he had performed, instructing a distraught mother to put her sick infant into a barrel of holy water to cure her consumption, and not a whimper out of the people when it died three days later, of pneumonia. A long way from the Carn of the Turnpike Inn and the fluttering bunting.

The eyes of the Sacred Heart had looked kindly down on Cassie Keenan every night of her life as she knelt on the stone floor of the kitchen where her husband lay snoring, her whispers drifting like moths out into the silence as she pleaded with Him for a glimpse into the world to which He belonged, a world that was blue and never-ending, where her and her one wee Josie would fuse as one and nothing bad would touch them ever again.

And when he went away to the markets and fairs, she combed her daughter's hair and said a Hail Holy Queen into her ear for she knew that the kindness in the eyes on the picture above the fireplace was the only hope she had.

Even at the end, Josie's father had turned to those eyes and that face too, clawing at the grave as he cried out, "Don't take my Cassie away from me, please Jesus please give me my Cassie back."

But there was no reply then either, not a finger twitch, the same immobile stare, and somewhere beyond, her mother, pale and serene beneath a blue sky in a meadow that never ended, waiting for her daughter to come and be a part of her.

And when the Buyer Keenan called her to come to him in the days after her burial, she did not hear.

Cassie, Cassie can you hear me calling you come to me Cassie!

Cassie lay with her arms folded on her chest and if he called for all the days that would ever exist she would never hear him, and that was how the Sacred Heart made the Buyer Keenan sorry for all the wrongs he had perpetrated on her and his child.

His face loomed up before Josie, his bottom lip quivering. He reached out to her with an unsteady hand. "I didn't know pet. You were the apple of my eye. I swear I wouldn't do anything to hurt you. You don't know what it's like for a man. I'd kill myself dead if I thought I hurt you."

Josie tried to turn away from it, but then she thought of her classmates at school, all those frail bodies in patched dresses, grown now like herself to women and some of them already with her mother.

Was that where they were or was it all a dream? A blue and never-ending place? Or a handful of bones and a grinning skull, a stopover for worms under a cross on a hill outside the town. *Is that what you are Molloy? You're a long way from it now, with your flashlight shaking and your bitter words*. The side of Josie's face tightened and she stroked it to ease the pain.

The gas fire in the corner flickered. On the sideboard, Josie smiled in a London street, behind her the teeming crowds and flashing neon of the city. Her skirt was pulled tight against her behind, her bosom visible just above the neckline of her sweater. She held her sunglasses delicately in her right hand. In those days she was Gina Lollobrigida. She had flicked through a magazine and read that La Lollo had prayed to the Sacred Heart as a girl, and asked Him to send her a doctor husband, fame and a lovely daughter. And by the age of twenty-one, she owned a princely mansion and had married a millionaire. But the Sacred Heart was not so flush twice and she had to settle for a room in Moss Side where the club across the street played Connie Francis records into the small hours and, to the sound of girlish innocence, Josie stared at the ceiling as they travelled her body smelling of tobacco and guilt. Cassie was always in her mind at those times in a happy place that would not end, where her father smiled down, clean-shaven and said softly, "There's nothing, only goodness in this world and you Josie pet, you're the one and only apple of Willie Keenan's eye."

❦

She went into the bedroom and sat in front of the mirror. She brushed her hair and drew an arc over one eye with a pencil. She pouted. Mmmmm—ah! She stroked her profile. She thought of the pin-ups in the daily papers. Kittenish women curled up in straw. The way she had been when they smiled at her in a room above a Manchester bar.

She thought of the first night a Carn man had come to the cottage in the Hairy Mountains. Like Phil Brady of years before, a frail body soon to be invaded by the moloch of age. Standing in the doorway, a cigarette shaking in his hand. "Maybe I could come back another time . . ."

Josie *knew*.

And the word of her knowledge soon travelled among the old and lonely men of the town and its hinterland.

She gave them the dark womblike world they wanted, drew them further into the web of their own weakness which they hated but could not best, she took them into the corners of their souls best left alone. And anything she felt within herself, she kept hidden from them. Only once had it got the better of her, when one of them had drooled like an infant at her breast, taking the nipple in his mouth and crying *mama mama*.

She emptied her stomach into the sink that night crying, *Why please what makes them do it Jesus Christ sick—*

Since then, she kept their gnarled obsessions as far from her as she could.

But now as she thought of it, the disgust crept up on her from that time. She dabbed two powder spots on her cheeks and laughed. She told herself it was a laugh that couldn't lose. She laughed louder and tears came to her eyes. Then she stopped laughing altogether. She fell on the bed and tried to stop the feeling that was coming over her, that nothing was ever any good, that nothing would ever be any good again. It was a feeling she had come to know well, and when they started again, she felt her hands begin to shake. The voices crept up on her, in no hurry, whispering in the distance at the back of her mind.

Come in for your tea Josie—isn't our Josie a wee pet? He passed away an hour ago sister, the poor child she's as well to know nothing. Tell her he's gone on a holiday poor thing and her with no mother . . .

An acidic taste came into her mouth. She went to the dresser and took down the bottle. She emptied two of the capsules into her hand and washed them down with a vodka.

She stared out at the bending branches of the hazel that reached towards the wreck of the railway and the town and, as the wind whistled through the leaves, she held back any tears she felt rising and saw the sunlight on the river again as her mother stood on a bucket half-buried in the field and snipped the catkins cleanly with a pair of scissors, handing them down to her. She bunched them in her arms and smiled as her mother stepped down gingerly and wiped the yellow-ish motes from her apron before they set off once more for the town.

I might as well do it now, go to that place where you are, that blue place far away from here. I haven't a thing to lose in the town of Carn or the world.

Then the drug began to cloud around her and her hard-edged thoughts softened, all the blame and anger within her eased and she felt nothing as she repeated the words again and again. After spilling clay on the little hands and the little toes, there was nothing more to lose.

The clock ticked on the mantelpiece. Inky clouds drifted desultorily across the anaemic face of the moon. Josie waited until the second gentle tap came before she got up. The man in the doorway looked about him uneasily, clutching his cap. She did not speak, and when he did, terrified by the silence, the words blurted out of him. "I heard . . . a man you know told me . . ."

Josie smiled and said, "Come in."

She took his cap from him and led him inside. She poured a drink and handed it to him.

"You're very quiet," she said to him. The glass was unsteady in his hand.

"So you heard about me?"

She moved closer to him. "You're shy," she said in a soft voice.

The man nodded and turned away.

"Oh now, don't be like that."

She put her arms around his neck and kissed him on the nose. He reddened and she laughed. His fingers strayed on his cheek.

"What do you think of my house?" she said, in a deeper huskier voice.

"It's . . . it's a fine wee place . . ."

"And my wallpaper? Do you like that? I put it up all by myself." She looked deep into his eyes. "All by my little self. And the pictures . Look—Venice By Night. Venice—what would the likes of us know about Venice?"

She laughed mockingly and he sighed with relief. Josie went on, "We'd look well rowing up the river in one of them gon-doh-lahs, eh? Look, here's a picture more in our line. The Sacred Heart. Names here for all the family and a big space at the top for mammy and daddy. That'd be more for us now and never mind them swanky foreign places. Eh?"

She stared at him. He frowned and his eyes fell. Then all he could see were the red shadows of the Sacred Heart lamp as she breathed on his cheek. For a long time Josie did nothing, just stood there stroking the side of his face with her long red fingernail. His lips tightened, he tried to fight it off but each stroke whittled away his resistance. He wanted to collapse before her power. There was nothing he could do to stop her when she began removing his clothes, prolonging each movement as if to torment him. She ran her tongue along her bottom lip. The red shadows floated around her. He stood in the centre of the room like a pale sheared sheep. Josie stood back from him and stared. He whimpered. She stroked his shoulders gently, kneading the flesh. He began to cry.

"If my wife . . . you wouldn't tell? Would you?"

"Ssh." Josie put a finger to her lips.

She led him into the bedroom. She lay him on the bed and stood over him. The sound of her breathing filled the room. She began to remove her own clothing. Her dress swished to the floor. Her breasts fell. She straddled his body and began to massage the parchment of his back. Small quivers ran down his spine. She bent down and whispered into his ear. "What's your name? Mmm? Have you got a little name for me?"

"Pat," he stammered. "It's Pat . . . Pat Lacey—for the love of God tell no one . . ."

"I knew I'd seen you before. I saw you in the paper."

She ran her soothing fingers through his hair, occasionally giving it sharp little tugs. She could feel his heartbeart racing.

"Is this what he told you about? This is what you expected—isn't it?"

"For the love of God, don't breathe a word to anyone, I'll pay you anything you want . . ."

She saw the tears trickling from his eyes.

"I'm sorry—I don't mean to be like this."

He took out a handkerchief and wiped them. She ran her fingers through his hair.

"I'm not a bad man, Josie," he said. "I try to fight it. I know it's wrong. I have everything. A good family, a lovely daughter. There's nothing I want for. There's people in this town would die for me. But it isn't like they think it is. Sometimes it goes wrong, doesn't it? I loved her Josie. I loved her like any man should love a woman. But women can't understand everything about a man. Sometimes—sometimes something fades away. We don't argue. My wife and I . . . we don't lay a finger on each other. These things get inside my head Josie and I don't know how they get there. I never touched a woman until I was thirty years of age. That's the way it was when I was growing up. These things in my head—I try to stop them coming. But there are times I can't. They take me over. I think of you—the way you know. Like no other woman can. It's like I wake up out of a bad dream and then I'm here—in this house. It makes me afraid. If it ever gets out that I'm like this . . . Mr Cooney or the priest—if they found out Josie . . ."

He gripped her forearm fearfully. Josie smiled. "What would they do, Pat love? What would they do if they found out what you liked?"

Without warning she slapped him across the face. His tears stained the pink bedspread. Outside the wind howled. The bedsprings creaked. She stroked his forehead. She dried his tears with her sleeve.

"I don't know how it started. I was caught one time. I was only young, Josie. I didn't know. The priest—in the school—he caught me in the toilet. I had a picture. A picture of a woman. He caught me with it. I was half-naked there in the toilet and he caught me with it. It was like I told you—a bad dream. I came out of the dream and he was standing there. He pushed me out of the toilet. I fell. Then he took the picture and pushed it into my face—over and over again. He started kicking me. He couldn't stop himself, there was spit on his mouth. He just kept kicking. It did something to me that time. I know it did. He beat me because of her and he beat me till I couldn't stand. He was afraid of her and he took it out on me, Josie. He told me the picture would haunt me till the day I died. Maybe that's why I am the way I am, Josie."

"Ssh," Josie soothed.

"I know it wouldn't be like this if I was away someplace. Anywhere. I know Cooney doesn't give a curse for me. He uses people like me. I'm not stupid Josie. That's the only thing I ever did with my life—a football club. That's all I have. I should have left this town. I've lived here all my life. I never seen places. I never gave myself a chance. I should've left a long

time ago ... I saw nothing, Josie. The football club—
what is it? What is to me or anyone else?"

She touched the nape of his neck with her hand.
Hard pimples pocked the reddish skin. He trembled
as he wept on her chest.

Josie was cold. The wind rattled the window. For a
split second she stood outside of herself and looked
down, then turned away in horror from what she saw,
her tongue licking an old man's ear as she cooed,
"There there. Who's a little baba? Who's a little bitty-
baba?" and the sound of Pat Lacey's whimpering
increased as he covered his face with his hands to hide
out all the world.

VIII

In Carn Poultry Products, the procession of claws continued past Sadie Rooney, the glazed eyes of the inverted fowl fixed on the ceiling girders as the deejay ranted breathlessly from the wall speakers. Only occasionally did Sadie bother to cock her ear to catch the name of a singer or the position of a song in the charts. Across from her the frenzied topic of discussion was the forthcoming factory outing to Kilkenny. Fact and fiction overlapped as incidents from the past were embellished with glee. The removal of the foreman's trousers, the ducking of the office girl in the swimming pool. They shook their heads and wiped the tears from their eyes. Sadie smiled along with them but she knew only too well that they would eagerly disown it all in the morning and secretly longed for the day when they would toss the nylon overall in a corner, curse Farrell the foreman yet again and walk away from it all for the last time. Much of it Sadie no longer heard, but when Una Lacey announced her engagement over the metal whirr of the assembly line, her words went right through Sadie like well-aimed bullets. "We finally got around to it, Sadie. Are you not going to congratulate me? It was eighty pounds!"

Sadie stared at the proffered stone in a daze.

"Are you not going to say anything then?" said Una. The other girls clustered about her like starlings. Una spoke effusively of the new house they were going to buy on an estate which had just been completed on the edge of the town.

"Well Sadie," said Una wistfully, "did you ever think you'd see the day?"

On the way home that evening, no matter how she fought it, Sadie felt as if she had leprosy. The dread inside her would not subside and when her mother, casually placing a plate of salad before her on the table said, "You'll want to mind yourself now young lady that you're not left on the shelf. They're all wiping your eye. They'll all watch out for themselves, you can be sure of that. Lord bless us, how the time passes," she did not reply.

Lying awake at night, she saw herself standing along the wall in The Sapphire, her heart thumping as she prayed that when she took their hands and allowed herself to be led on to the floor that they would not smell of drink or talk mindlessly of football or farming. She no longer set her sights high, afraid now in her own mind to challenge Una's words when she spoke of the days of the Golden Chip and Dave Robinson ("Hadn't we little sense?"). And despite herself, she knew she was now approaching what she had always feared, a time when any kind of warmth would do. Whenever any memories of the

Golden Chip came back, she did not dwell on them, leaving them to recede without pursuit. Whenever there was any mention of that time in the company of others, she raised her eyes up to heaven like the rest, disowning all involvement.

When the outing came, she linked arms at the back of the bus and sang boisterously along with the communal songs. She got drunk on lagers in a pub not far from the castle they had visited and put her arms around a girl who said, "How did I used to think you were stuck up?"

She went with them to The Sapphire on Saturday nights and like them stood clutching a cigarette packet outside the toilet, hunted eyes flitting about the hall as they evaluated social status and personal hygiene. She fixed her hair anxiously, holding pins between her lips and examining acne blemishes in detail, no longer listening to the tiny whispers in her head that said, "Sadie—Sadie. What are you doing here? Do you hear me Sadie?"

As she circled the floor of the The Sapphire, she rested her hands on the shoulders of her partners and looked away, struggling to endure the fumes of drink and the mindless babble of local affairs. She sat with them in parked cars, lay beneath them on coarse upholstery or against the pebbledash of a wall as they travelled her body like bears in the safety of darkness. She anaesthetised herself so that her true feelings would not emerge and word travel back to the factory where she would find herself standing alone again. She did not hear when they said, fumbling with their clothing, "They're getting good bands here now," or "They're doing a lot of building on Church Hill."

She came home every Saturday night with the sound of hissing cymbals in her ears. She made herself toast and tea and sat listening to Radio Luxembourg. She remained there until there was nothing in her mind except a steady repetitive buzz. Then she went upstairs and fell into a deep sleep from which she didn't care if she ever woke.

Una Lacey had her reception in the Turnpike Inn. It was a double event for her father and mother were celebrating their twenty-fifth wedding anniversary that very day. And the council had decided to make a presentation to Mr and Mrs Pat Lacey on this occasion.

Beneath the balloon-decked ceiling, the priest stood in the centre of the floor and whipped off his jacket, urging everyone both young and old to join in. Una Lacey and her new husband were ushered out for the hokey-cokey. The men at the bar uttered mild vulgarities behind their hands, guffawing loudly to themselves. They stared at Josie Keenan who had wandered in off the street and was brazenly surveying the proceedings from the corner of the bar. Then they looked away sharply lest they should make eye contact with her.

John F. Kennedy smiled benignly down on everyone.

Streamers flew wildly and whistles rent the air. Sadie was making her way back from the dance floor when she felt a hand on her shoulder and she turned to face Benny Dolan. She was taken aback when he asked her to dance and she became flustered and tried to stammer a reply. But they were already caught in the surge of dancers and there was nothing she could do but go with it. She was even further taken aback when Benny Dolan did not speak of mundane local affairs but of his biking holiday in Turkey with Joe Noonan, whose sister worked with her in the factory. He talked non-stop and Sadie found herself laughing as he gestured and mimicked tales of their travels. When the dance ended, he put his arm around her waist and said, "A drink maybe?" Sadie nodded, reddening a little. They sat down and he ordered a drink. They began their conversation anew by swopping acquaintances and experiences from work but then they got on to music and travel. For the first time in a long time, Sadie Rooney began to feel at ease. Joe Noonan joined them for a while. He squeezed Sadie's arm and said, "Whatever he tells you, believe none of it. It's all lies. Istanbul? The furthest he ever got was the school trip to Cavan."

Sadie's head eased itself onto Benny's shoulder. The priest sailed past red-cheeked, clutching at his flailing jacket. The middle-aged woman beside them leaned over and said to Sadie, bleary-eyed, "Who's the lucky girl then?"

"Una Lacey," replied Sadie. "A friend of mine."

"Lacey? Did you say Lacey?"

Sadie nodded. The woman frowned and pursed her

lips. She was somewhat the worse for drink and had been muttering to herself. "Lacey," she said under her breath.

Just then there was a roll of drums and a microphone whistled. A burly man with a red face introduced himself as Jack Murphy, the secretary of the council and lifelong friend of Mr Lacey's. He fumbled with his notes and began to speak. He said that today was a very special occasion and that, although it was somewhat unorthodox, he and his colleagues had felt that it was appropriate to take this opportunity to honour one of Carn's finest families. He praised Mr and Mrs Lacey to the skies and said that he hoped that now Una was getting married there would be many more Laceys. This was greeted with wild cheers. He cleared his throat and continued. He went on to say that in the past few years, Pat Lacey had almost single-handedly revived the fortunes of Carn Rovers Football Club to the extent that they were now one of the finest teams in the country. They had brought great honour not only to the town but to the county also.

He then called on Mr Lacey to come forward and accept the silver platter as a gift from the council and the people of the town to himself and his wife on the occasion of their twenty-fifth wedding anniversary. There was a mighty cheer and the priest clapped louder than any. Pat Lacey stood on the stage, somewhat embarrassed. He coughed and adjusted the microphone. He said that he was astounded, that he had done nothing to deserve such a presentation. He was at a loss for words, he said. It was not he but the people of the town themselves who had revived the dormant spirit of Carn Rovers FC. And in particular men like Father Kelly and James Cooney who had given so much of their time and energy. Whistles rent the air. No, continued Pat Lacey, Carn had the best club and the finest club in the whole province. He accepted the silver platter and, turning once more to the eager assembly, raised his arm and said, "Remember—this is the year Carn leaves all other towns behind. Here We Go Carn!" Hats were flung in the air, streamers flew wildly. They clapped and cheered as the band struck up a rousing medley.

The woman beside Sadie had moved in among them. She was still smiling to herself. Her lips went in and out as she mumbled half-sentences. She leaned over to Sadie and said something but she did not catch it and looked around her awkwardly. But Benny stepped in and said, "How's things out by the railway? Aren't you in the cottage?"

Josie smiled and nodded.

"I'm going to the bar. Do you both want a drink?"

"Yes," Sadie replied.

She got into conversation with the woman who gave her her life story. She had lived a long time in England. Sadie was beginning to warm to her as she continued, although much of what she said was rambling and disjointed. She dropped ash on Sadie's dress as she said, "My father died when I was young. I left here when I was sixteen. I left here when I was your age."

"First chance I get, I'm going too. I'm going to do a

secretarial course. You can get work over there no problem."

"You'll do better than I did. That wouldn't be hard." Her head lolled as she steered the cigarette to her lips.

"I was thinking of studying at night and getting some kind of qualification."

"Carn manages to get rid of the young ones, one way or another," said the woman.

"What's your name?" asked Sadie. "Have you still got people about the town?"

"Josie Keenan. The only people I have are in the graveyard above."

"I'm sorry," Sadie said and rose as Benny returned with the drinks.

He took the woman's drunkenness in his stride. "Oh you'll have to watch that landlord of yours. He owns two hundred acres and he wouldn't give you a tosser."

"Move over there," interrupted Joe Noonan as he sat down and swigged from his drink.

Josie was accepted into the company and talked a long time to Sadie about the change in Carn.

"I don't see much change," said Sadie, laughing, "apart from Blast Morgan's new overalls."

The drink flowed.

Josie sang along with them as they linked arms and chorused, "For he's a jolly good fellow, for he's a jolly good fellow . . ."

Una Lacey came over trailing her train and bade them all goodnight. They blew kisses at her. They were still singing when Una's father approached with his hand extended, saying goodbye to everyone. When he saw Josie his face went deathly pale. He stumbled against a chair and turned to cross the hall. Josie looked away and went to the ladies toilet. He stood with his back to her, trying to conceal his quivering lip with his hand. As Josie returned, one of the guests, a member of the Tidy Towns Committee, said to Pat Lacey, "I say Pat—who's that there? I haven't seen her before . . . who invited her?"

Every nerve in Pat Lacey's body tightened. He stood frozen to the spot. "I don't know," he repeated drymouthed. "I don't know."

The other man shrugged his shoulders, disorientated by Pat Lacey's reaction. Then he called to one of the waitresses and disappeared into the swaying crowd.

The carousing went on until late. Josie left the Turnpike with the others. They stood in the main street, still singing. Josie told them they were all welcome out in the Hairy Mountains any time. Joe Noonan put his arm around her and said she was one of the best, even if she had a bit of an English accent. As they stood there the warm breeze fanned their cheeks.

"We'll have to meet again Josie," Sadie said, "I really enjoyed that."

"We'll arrange it soon, okay?" interrupted Benny.

"*We'll meet again . . .*" sang Joe Noonan, staggering against a lamppost.

"*Who knows where who knows when . . .*" answered Josie.

"Right then," said Benny, "be seeing you, okay?"

Josie walked to the corner with Joe Noonan and then set off towards the railway where the Hairy Mountains rose up in the distance like black tidal waves.

Sadie got up on the pillion of Benny's motorbike and they spent an hour cruising the back roads of Carn. "Some bike, eh Sadie?" cried Benny against the wind.

"Fabulous," replied Sadie.

When they got back to the town the Golden Chip was still open and they went in for a coffee to sober up. "Tell me more about your travelling," said Sadie. Benny's eyes narrowed and with a mischievous glint he put his arm around her neck and said, "We'll travel the world together you and me. The back of a Kawasaki all the way to Katmandu."

And the more they talked, the further Sadie drifted away from the deadening whirr of the assembly line and by the time they left the café, she felt she had known Benny Dolan a long long time.

They stood together outside her house. "I want to talk to you all I can," she said. She stared up at the stars and felt his warm breath on her neck. She was up there with them, far from Carn and in that instant it all came back to her, the way it had been in the Golden Chip, all those days came at once and she felt a surge of energy running through her. She stroked his face and said, "Benny. Oh Benny."

He quivered a little and said, "I've always fancied you Sadie . . ."

"Benny. We could go anywhere . . ."

"Anywhere," replied Benny. "Anywhere."

And they sat on the window-sill until first light of dawn and Sadie awoke on his shoulder and smiled as she watched a sparrow trot along the paling fence at the bottom of Mr Galvin's garden.

IX

When Northern Ireland erupted shortly afterwards, Maisie Lynch blamed drugs.

She parroted the news bulletins verbatim at the giblet counter, addressing an imaginary audience in wounded tones, claiming that she had seen it coming for years and that her repeated warnings had been consistently ignored. "You can't expect anything else when you fly in the face of God," she cried.

She accosted Benny Dolan regularly and snapped at him, "Well—what does your father think of all this carry-on in the north now? All this bombing and killing? He could tell you all about it! But there was none of that in the old days! There were decent men then. No killing children or old people then!"

At first Benny paid her no attention but as the reports coming through became more disturbing, he grew impatient with her and, on the morning after the first British soldier had been shot in the province, she approached him reciting a scribbled prayer she had written, "For all the poor people in the north who are killed by guns and bombs O Lord we pray that they may live in peace and harmony, free from pain and trouble and strife and drugs and those who fly in Thy face. Hear our prayers, Lord, we beseech Thee." She stood in front of Benny defiantly. When he pushed impatiently past her, she stood in the centre of the yard and called after him, "Go on then! Pay no heed! You're as bad as any of them! Your father blew up the custom-hut!"

❦

The situation across the border went from bad to worse after that. The television screens were filled with images of burning barricades and crouched squaddies at street corners. Mobs outside burning terraced houses. Distraught women clutching mystified infants. In the meat plant canteen, the workers were stunned into silence by the story of three young Scottish soldiers who were lured from a public house to their deaths. Then when news came through of the British Army's behaviour in the Catholic areas of Belfast, vengeance was sworn. Fists were clenched in the Turnpike Inn, the republican songs resounded bitterly. A number of Belfast men came to work in the factory, bringing with them tales of assassination and burnings, of horrific beatings and torture at the hands of the authorities. These men, because of what they had endured, for a time were almost worshipped. It was considered an honour to buy them a drink. They brought their own songs with them, beside which the older ballads favoured by the Carn men seemed insipid and outdated. The Turnpike Inn was filled with the sound of *The Sniper's Promise* and *The Weary Provo*. Benny became very friendly with one of the northmen, having spent a fortnight with him in the boning hall, listening to him describe how he had been pistol-whipped in front of his wife and children, his house torn asunder before the soldiers left, spitting on a family photograph as they went, vowing to find evidence the next time they came. At home, Benny and his father spoke of little else. Everything the older man had told him in the past now began to clarify itself in his mind.

"She's going up again, Benny," he said, "only this time it'll be the final roundup. It should have been finished fifty years ago but it'll be finished this time for sure."

They talked long into the small hours about the history of the state and events in the north since its inception. His father told him the story of his uncle who was arrested by the police on Christmas day in the fifties, stripped naked and held without charge in a prison cell, taunted by the bored policemen who told them they had lifted him "Just in case he might do something sometime."

Over a period of time, Benny became obsessed with the subject and spent a lot of time in the company of the northmen who were taken by his knowledge and sincerity.

Joe Noonan too became infected by this new passion.

Gradually the enthusiasm with which they had

spoken of motorbikes, music and travel began to recede, supplanted by angry outbursts against the army and the security forces in the six counties. They often went north, spending weekends with the factory northmen in their homes in Belfast and Derry.

"Brit bastards" fell from their lips with ease. Republican stickers and tricolours adorned their bikes.

This new development dislocated Sadie Rooney. Often she now found herself on the edge of the conversation staring in at something she did not understand. When she attempted to involve herself, her lack of conviction showed and led only to awkward, temporary silences. So on many occasions she sat there without comment as the arguments and debates took on lives of their own. She began to realise that a new uneasiness had taken hold of her. Benny had not mentioned their planned leavetaking for several months. She did want to broach the subject this time. She felt it was now up to him.

The old tensions began to insinuate themselves. She awoke at odd times in the night. She told herself that it couldn't happen again, not now, and revisited many of the times that they had had together since they met. But as time wore on, she began to admit to herself that things were not the same. There was no talk between them now of music, of frivolity of any kind. The new obsession had engulfed all that. Shootings, hijackings, rubber bullets, provos, stickies, Carson, Paisley, taigs, the meaningless catalogue ran through her head every night after they had been together.

She began to feel as if she were intruding on Benny and Joe Noonan. They no longer spoke directly to her, the northmen often talking behind their hands in her presence, as if they quietly disapproved of her. Finally one night, when her anxiety had backed her into a corner, Sadie blurted out nervously, "Benny— are you going to give in your notice or are you not?"

Benny looked away and ran his fingers through his hair. He pulled her close to him. Then he looked at her and with honesty in his face said, "I can't. Not now. We'll have to wait and see what happens."

She looked at him and felt nothing. "That's it then," she said as they stood there outside her house, listening to the rattle of the torn chicken wire at the bottom of Mr Galvin's garden.

Some weeks later, she told him of her pregnancy without any hysterics. He did not say anything, just passed his motorbike helmet from hand to hand as if he had somehow forgotten who she was.

In her cottage in the Hairy Mountains, Josie Keenan answered the telephone to hear Pat Lacey's voice at the other end of the line. "Josie—I need to see you. Please! Can I come out? Please say I can come out, Josie . . ."

Josie soothed him as he cried, her mind far away as the rain dribbled down the window pane.

And not long after that, the town of Carn froze when it heard how Blast Morgan had lifted a bundle of rags in the doorway of the Home Bakery and cursing, "Bloody tinkers, never clean up after them," had tossed it into his bin before being blown twenty feet across the street with half his stomach hanging out.

Part Two

X

It was some years later.

The Christmas tree swung into place and its roped branches unfurled like wings across the The Diamond. Jack Murphy, the secretary of Carn Council, stood back and mopped his brow, observing it from every angle like a photographer gauging a shot. "She's a beauty," he said, and the other members of the council concurred, taking this as the signal to break into animated conversation about the tasks that still faced them. There was the Meals on Wheels Jumble Sale; the Fire Brigade Party for the itinerants; the annual Dinner Dance; and of course the Christmas party for the old folks. "No rest for the wicked," laughed the chairman as he rubbed his hands with a cloth and set off across The Diamond.

Christmas bells were ringing in Carn.

There was snow above on the hill where the lights of the meat plant twinkled merrily as the noise of squealing beasts tumbled out across the fields of the hinterland. In the Sacred Heart Church, the baby Jesus was snug in his crib and the candles were being lit for midnight Mass. Carols jingled in the shops. Alec Hamilton's Five-Star Supermarket was lit up like a ship and had no intention of closing until well after ten. Alec Hamilton himself stood in the doorway in his brown coat welcoming all his customers personally and wishing them a merry festive season. Not to be outdone the new Hypermarket across the road was raffling no less than ten turkeys. There had been dances for the past four nights in The Sapphire Ballroom. The Golden Chip restaurant had undergone complete refurbishment and was now called Pete's Pizza Parlour, its dayglo menus advertising the best in hamburgers and mouth-watering pizzas specially prepared by Sergio who now wore a striped uniform with a name badge on the chest.

Dusty snow fell on the slated rooftops of Dolan Square where the neatly-painted black letters commemorated the valiant deeds of Matt Dolan. The windows of the upstairs lounge in the Turnpike Inn lit up suddenly and music blared out into the main street as Dekko and his Jetflite Disco began his evening stint. At the counter James Cooney stood with his chin resting on his hand as a worker insisted, "You and me were at school together James. You had the brains. Not many saw it then but I knew it all along. Without you where would this town be? On the rubbish tip, that's where James."

On the wall Davy Crockett had a sprig of holly pinned to his nose. John F. Kennedy was criss-crossed with flags. The huge video screen at the back blared incessantly. There was an insatiable demand for the mince pies from the microwave.

MERRY CHRISTMAS TO ONE AND ALL read the cardboard letters above the entrance.

And the Christmas tree, bedecked with coloured bulbs, looked down over all from the centre of the The Diamond, as they swarmed from the disco and The Sapphire to the Yankee Doodle Burger House and Pete's Pizza Parlour and then towards home, the snow covering their tracks as Francie Mohan fell across the square shouting about the boat train and the brown paper parcel. Then the lights went off in the Turnpike Inn and James Cooney checked the doors again before saying goodnight to his staff and sliding into his BMW.

His new mansion three miles outside the town was the envy of all, with its swimming pool, jacuzzi and pillars like a Greek temple.

The factory was poised like a puma on the hill, ready for action at six-thirty and not a minute later.

In the town hall, Pat Lacey, since chosen as Mayor of Carn in two successive elections, finished off his meeting with Father Kelly who had privately come to his house on a number of occasions in order to persuade him to become secretary of the newly founded Anti-Divorce League. The priest felt that a man of his popularity could do much to influence the people and hold back the insidious tide of alien values and beliefs that was threatening to destroy the traditional way of life in Carn and in Ireland as a whole.

He visited constantly until Pat Lacey had little choice but to consent. So now, after this latest meeting, Pat Lacey was not only the President of

Carn Rovers FC and the Mayor of Carn, but was now the official secretary of the Carn branch of The Anti-Divorce League.

Then Carn turned over in its bed, checked the money in its pocket and went off to sleep as happy as it had ever been, the little spot of bother with the bomb some years back already fading into memory.

There was one man in the town who had of late acquired a profile almost as high as that of James Cooney.

That was JR Ewing, the dude rancher and oil magnate from Dallas, Texas. Almost every conversation, no matter what the subject, managed to include a reference to him or his family at some stage. There were very few who did not tune in weekly to catch up on his mischievous deeds in the world of high finance, and those who vowed they wouldn't be caught dead watching often sneaked the odd private look into his glittering world. He split the town in two. One half loved him and the other hated him. They spoke of the characters as if they were real living flesh and blood. The toyshops and newsagents were filled with portraits, magazines and souvenirs relating to the Ewing family. Their white mansion beamed from the window of The Hypermarket. The back windows of cars sported triangular stickers which queried *Who loves JR Ewing?* The daily newspapers carried stories of their social and sexual exploits which were devoured with glee and the Sunday supplements were eagerly awaited as they often ran stories which were lavishly illustrated with photographs of the interior of the Ewing mansion. They took away the breath of the people who lived in The Park and The Terrace.

On their way home from the butcher's, Sadie listened without interruption as Benny's mother breathlessly outlined the story of the most recent episode. Sadie nodded at the appropriate intervals. By the time they reached the house, she had got on to Coronation Street and the most recent atrocity in the north. Sadie did not interrupt her flow. Since the blistering row they had had over Josie's babysitting Tara, she wanted to keep their exchanges as anaemic and neutral as possible. She winced as she recalled the older woman's bitterness. "Do you know who that woman is, do you? Do you know who you're letting into your house, do you? Have you no sense, letting her near your child? Benny, for God's sake talk sense into her . . ."

She had persisted until Sadie, worn out and for the sake of peace, had been forced to decline Josie's persistent offers until it dawned on her and she no longer made it her business to pass by Abbeyville Gardens on her visits to the town. When they met on the street, conversation between them now was stilted and awkward. "Why do you never call now?" Sadie said. "Too busy," Josie laughed, "haven't a minute to myself." But Sadie knew. And she knew. And it made Sadie feel sick when she thought of it.

"There's not much sense in me waiting until Benny gets home. God knows what time he'll be off that nightshift. The sooner that stops the better."

She kissed the sleeping child on the forehead and Sadie saw her to the door. She watched as she went down the road and turned the corner to the Jubilee Terrace where Sadie's old house lay idle since her mother's death. Her mother-in-law faded from sight and Sadie shrugged. She went inside and made herself a coffee. She switched on the television but there was nothing on any channel but football. Although she had no interest in it she left it on and sat drinking her coffee, waiting for the first sign of a stir from Tara. The terrace crowd chanted as she staved off her growing unease. She had nothing to complain about, she told herself. Nothing. What was she worrying about? What could she have done about Josie? Mrs Dolan would have gone on and on and on about it. There was nothing else she could have done. She did it for the sake of peace.

No, she had nothing to complain about. Things had improved in the last year. It wasn't like it had been. Not remotely. Then it had been hard. She had never dreamed then she'd come this far.

That day on their honeymoon in The Atlantic Hotel. Benny sitting on the edge of the bed smoking a cigarette and staring out the open window at the ocean. "It'll be all right," she said, "won't it Benny?" He turned to her and laid a hand on her forearm. "It's going to be okay Sadie," he said. "It just took us by surprise, that's all."

After that, when they had returned, the shadow of

Mrs Dolan hovered about the house at all hours. Bootees and small cardigans piled up in cupboards and women stopped her in the street regaling her with stories of pregnancies past and present. "For God's sake," said a former colleague from the factory, "don't go to Doctor Patton—he gave our Mary a turned-in foot."

Faces lit up as they uttered the words "colic", "uterus" and "heartburn". She had begun to swell and she felt Benny drawing away from her. She knew it was through no fault of his own, perplexed by these things women had made their own, with whispered talk of "cystitis", "lactations" and "backache".

She lay tense in the night watching the moon on the bedroom window and slowly coming to the realisation that things were never going to be the same again. She had strange dreams. Of herself in stirrups with whitecoated doctors sawing and pulling out of her as she felt its squirming body wrenched away from her, looking down to see the grotesque head of a devil. She had behaved erratically at that time, bursting into tears while sweeping the kitchen or standing staring into space while shopping in the supermarket. Una called regularly to console her. "Never mind those scaremongers," she said, "they'll tell you everthing but the good news. You can be sure of that. I had our John in an hour. Out he popped like a cork. You won't know yourself afterwards." But when Sadie's turn came, her daughter didn't pop out like a cork. She was taken to hospital two weeks early and had to lie unattended for hours at a time in a lime green ward surrounded by glum women who stroked the mountains of their bellies and leafed sullenly through magazines. When the contractions started, she floated through space and the only sound she heard from the earth was the squeaking of wheels on a trolley as they led her into a gleaming silver ward. They laid her on a table and in her own mind lying there she went for Benny Dolan in The Atlantic Hotel and clawed at him with her fingernails as she cried bitterly, "You did this to me. You did this and it's all for nothing. I hate you. I hate you! I never loved you!"

Faces loomed but she spat at them too and the sweat streamed onto the pillow until the calm came and she looked up to see a nurse with the infant cradled in her arms.

After that she had opened out like a flower and those days were the happiest of her life. Joe Noonan had arrived in the ward somewhat the worse for drink and presented her with a bunch of sorry-looking carnations. Benny kissed her on the cheek and said, "I told you it'd be okay, pet" Mrs Dolan busied herself by the bedside, changing the baby authoritatively, tidying magazines. Sadie felt she was in good hands and the days stretched out warmly before her.

Then, on the last day of her stay in hospital, after she had said goodbye to all her afternoon visitors, she found herself sitting erect in the bed as if she were hanging on a cliff edge. She wanted to cry out for help and she didn't know why. Her body felt drained and dragged. The infant's squeal pierced her head. Everyone was gone. She was on her own. Tears rolled down her cheeks and she was inconsolable, the nurses looking at each other, perplexed.

But the feeling passed and when she arrived home with the baby wrapped in the shawl Una gave her, she felt protected and warm again. A fire burned in the hearth and her own mother and Mrs Dolan had chops grilling. Benny greeted her in the doorway. "Tara," he said, "We'll call her Tara." She began to feel it had all been some sort of temporary aberration, some inexplicable malfunction of her disturbed body, the reaction of confused hormones. It would never return again.

But it did.

Some weeks later, when all had settled and the routine of the day was once more established, she was sitting feeding the baby, cooing to it, when out of nowhere, the feeling slid down over her like an invisible skin. Her hands began to shake. The child cried. Her whole body seemed to be stained with the smell of the baby. Her dressing gown was completely covered in small white pools of its sick. She felt as if they were breeding on her and would drive her mad. The baby continued crying. She shook it violently to stop it but it only became more frantic. Then she was consumed by guilt over what she'd done. "Help me Benny," she cried aloud. "Please Benny I can't stand it."

She waited for some kind of answer from thin air. Outside the window, birds sang on a telephone wire. A child tossed a red ball into the air and raced across the park, calling. She could hear the television in the house next door. She just lay down before the feeling that had come upon her, its terrible weight pressing tears from her eyes as the child kicked its legs, demanding everything she had to give from Sadie.

The feeling came and went over the next few years. She never knew when it would come. It was as if she were under siege, threatened by an enemy whose face she could not make out in the darkness. She tried to talk to Benny about it but often his work had drained him too and when he did listen, he explained it away by saying, "It takes time. It'll work itself out. It's common Sadie."

Gradually Sadie began to feel that such feelings were part and parcel of the whole arrangement and that she was being unreasonable in complaining about it.

The only one who could begin to understand was Una but she could only counterfeit a kind of empathy as she had been in and out of hospital in two days and had experienced nothing as severe as Sadie's feelings.

"I'm sure it will pass in time," she said. "Isn't that what it says in these books?"

Unable to battle the unpredictability of her emotions alone, Sadie often woke up in the night in a state of dread, anticipating the cry of the baby and the oncoming blackness. When it came upon her in the middle of the day, she gave herself to the television, let it whisk her mind where it would, for anything was preferable to facing the thoughts her own mind thrust upon her. She just wanted away from what waited inside herself.

Much of the day she passed in this fashion, sitting in her dressing gown with the child slumbering on her lap and a cup of coffee always at her elbow. The frenetic voices of quizmasters and childern's presenters rang out throughout the morning.

A year went by and slowly the skin began to peel from her. She dressed earlier in the day, drank less coffee and paid less heed to the flickering screen. Her daughter had grown a beautiful shock of blonde hair and was a star turn with her blubbering attempts at "da da". Visitors adored her huge blue saucer eyes. Sadie felt gladdened when locals stopped her in the street and plucked the child's cheek, examining her for family resemblances.

When she missed a period the second time, she was filled so full of disbelief that she nearly burst out laughing. She told no one because she was convinced it was so ridiculous. She reeled inside herself. Then she drank gin. Bottles of it. Benny had been stunned to find her lying by the fireplace and the child soiled, screaming. He told her to get a grip of herself.

Before she knew where she was, they were gathering around her again and congratulating her on her enthusiasm. When she met the girls from the factory in the street, they crossed over and said, "I hear you're about to go again. You'll have your hands full now. But it'll be great company for Tara." Her mother squeezed her shoulder and said, "Ah, it's not so bad, daughter, one will rear the other."

The litany began again—nightfeed, lactations, colic . . .

But this time she heard none of it. Benny was delighted and gave her more flowers. Joe Noonan sent her a card. "Another wee Dolan stalks the land Sadie," was written on it.

But that was as close as either of them came to the child for Benny was too embarrassed to over-involve himself. To him it was women's work. Her work. In the street, he touched the buggy uncertainly with one hand, his awkward fingers buttoning the baby clothes half-heartedly.

The child was born but this time the admirers did not linger. "The second one is different," her mother said. "People have their lives to lead Sadie." That was the way it was and the way it was going to be for Sadie, and she knew that.

And now there were two of them.

At the back of her mind the future unrolled itself in a fog for Sadie did not want to stare at it

There's nothing I can do about it now, it was saying. *There's nothing left now. Just forget about everything, everything belongs to them now.*

She went outside to leave out the milkbottles. A light snow was falling. Children's toys lay abandoned on lawns. A car turned into the estate, churning slush onto the sidewalk. A woman in a powder-pink tracksuit waved. Lights glimmered in the living rooms. At the end of the estate a sign read *Please Mind Our Children Drive Slowly*.

The lights of another car rose up. Sadie sighed. A neighbour turned a key in a door, looked awkwardly in her direction, then went inside. A neighbour. Like Mr Galvin years before. *But times have changed Mr Galvin, neighbours like ghosts now, you catch them on a summer day in the back garden if you're lucky. Nothing now only the click of the plug next door and Saturday morning car talk.*

Is that you Sadie? Sadie Rooney? said Mr Galvin looking up from his ridges. *I thought you'd be halfway across the world by now. So you're still in the town of Carn. Well boys oh boys. Lord above isn't the world a strange place and me here thinking all the time you were in Carnaby Street or some place.*

No. I never bothered going to London, Mr Galvin. I don't suppose I'll be able to make it now that I have the pair of them.

Sadie, daughter, don't tell me you have your own now?

I have, Mr Galvin, Tara and Darren, moving on now the pair of them.

Well doesn't the time pass, eh? Wee Sadie Rooney. So you never went to London. Isn't that a good one now?

I'll hardly make it now, do you think so Mr Galvin?

No, I daresay you won't but aren't you as well off above there in Abbeyville Gardens? I hear you have great neighbours up there.

Neighbours is right. The best of neighbours. Mr JR Ewing and Dusty and Sue Ellen and Blake Carrington and Alexis and Jeff and Cliff Barnes and Jason Colby and Bet Lynch and Hilda Ogden, they all live up beside me Mr Galvin. Did you never hear of JR Mr Galvin? Of course you did.

Sue Ellen?

Yeah.

You lawv me Sue Ellen?

Shuah Jay Aw.

You shuah you lawv me?

Shuah Jay Aw.

You kin have anythang, anythang you want.

Oh Jay Aw Jay Aw.

Oh to tell you the truth Sadie, I wouldn't know what the hell a lad like that would be talking about.

You know what the woman next door says Mr Galvin?

What would that be Sadie?

She says, "You know I think they're as good as any neighbours those programmes. And they don't nosey into your business like some people. Even though you can spy all you like on them."

So they're your neighbours, Sadie. Isn't it well for you has neighbours the like of that.

Well for you.

It was true, wasn't it?

No one else complains, thought Sadie. And as her mother had said long ago, who did she think she was—someone special? Who did she think she was— JR Ewing?

She went inside. Outside another car passed, its lights swallowing up the room. Then all settled back to silence. A plug clicked in the wall next door. The snow drifted past the window pane and Sadie sat where she was, staring into space as the tears rolled down her cheeks and a frenzied voice in the corner of her living room, uncertain of its origins, wavered between American and Irish inflections as it promised more than a lifetime's service from a new brand of motor car . . .

XI

Maisie Lynch looked up from the packed crate and called to Benny Dolan, "I saw them below at Cooney's new discotheque last night. Every one of them full of drink, and the women the worst. Hail Mary full of Grace my backside Benny, lie through your teeth, keep up the front and rob your neighbour blind." Then she closed one eye and leaned across whispering, "Did you hear about this terrible business last night? They tried kill that fellow from Belfast. Drove up to his house and tried to shoot him stone dead in his own house. You'll remark there's no sign of him today. That's what happened, did you not hear? But I'll have nothing to do with it. Say nothing, that's the best policy, they're all a bad crowd Benny. They're all mixed up in it, these northmen. Your father was a good man, there's nobody can say any different about Hugo Dolan. Wasn't he up on the platform with the minister the time of the commemorations?"

Benny heard nothing she said. But the incident had been on his mind all morning. The man concerned had only recently come from Belfast to work in the boning hall and was staying with relatives six miles outside the town. Benny pieced the uncertain fragments together. He had been playing cards with an old couple who lived nearby. *Scots accents*, it was rumoured, *and a Brit, upperclass, officer*. Benny knew the area well. He could see it. The car driving silently across the unapproved road. Four, maybe six men in the car, nobody could know that yet. A house somewhere on the Carn side where they collected their weapons. The car parked in a layby. Up ahead lights burning in a cottage, a gate swinging in a field, the car door opening and the men making their way across the field to the cottage. The front door kicked open, the old couple staring at them in horror. The northman producing a gun from nowhere and diving for the back door. The would-be assailants stricken with panic, the old couple huddling in a corner waiting for their death. A Scottish voice shouting out into the night. The wall sprayed with bullets. Then chaos, the car door slamming, the engine revved off towards the nothern side. There had been rumours since the summer of an organised gang carrying out raids on the southern side with back up from the British army. A number of local men had disappeared. One of them had been mysteriously transported across the border and his hooded body found weeks later in a culvert. On every occasion there had been a mention of English and Scottish accents.

The northman had escaped, but was badly wounded in the stomach. The early morning news bulletin had described it as an internal paramilitary feud.

"Do you agree with me?" quizzed Maisie, looking into his eyes.

The hooter sounded for break. Benny lit up a cigarette and sat on a crate with his sandwiches. His rib twinged again. It had been cracked the previous week at the march. He had said nothing about it to Sadie. What was the point in her knowing, only upset her. Joe had been lucky, got out clean as a whistle.

"That's only a scratch, Dolan," the policeman had said bitterly. "Next time I'll fix it for you good and proper."

Benny had gone with the northmen from the factory, standing in a field waiting for the helicopter to land with the coffin of the dead hunger striker. Beneath the whirring rotor blade, four special branch men had appeared with the coffin on their shoulders. They carried it across the field and over a wall into the churchyard. Their colleagues watched with Uzzi machine guns slung by their sides. The shuttered streets were lined with blue-clad policemen, figures from a futuristic film with visors and riot shields. They stood ominously in front of sweetshops tapping batons as the protestors strained towards the steel barriers. Suddenly the barriers had buckled and Benny found himself swept along on a wave of bodies and in a split second pinned down by his arms as a baton resounded thickly against his ribs. The white face of the young policeman stared tensely down at him, the baton shaking in his hand. Later they had marched morosely past the closed pubs and curtained windows as a piper played a lament and the colour party moved, in dark glasses and berets, at the front.

As they stood in silence in the cemetery, an army helicopter droned overhead, soldiers dotted the surrounding hills like dolls wound up and ready for action. A young notherner, overcome, had broken from the crowd and confronted a policeman crying, "Free State Pigs!" to be dragged off cursing to a waiting van. This was too much for some of the northmen and vicious scuffles broke out between them and the police. Stones were thrown. A tricolour and a Union Jack were simultaneously burnt. Joe Noonan spat at a soldier, "Imperialist scum."

The crowds in the town did not disperse until well after dark. Police reinforcements arrived by the hour.

On the coach home, the exhausted marchers sang *The Boys of the Old Brigade*.

The radio carried an appeal from a bishop to all the young men of Ireland. He called on them to renounce violence. He castigated patriotic songs and said they spoke of nothing but guns and bloodshed. We have had enough of this revolutionary mythology, he said, far too many young men of twenty had gone out to die. He called on everyone north and south not to be afraid to stand up and be counted. We must root out this Frankenstein of evil in our midst. After all, they cannot shoot us all.

The bus cheered loudly as the bishop concluded and another song was struck up with renewed gusto.

The police called at Benny's house on two occasions after that, "making routine checks". The detective smiling and saying as they left, "I knew your father Hugo well. Did you not see me at his funeral? Me and him used to have long chats below in the barracks. I'm sure he'd be pleased to see you're following in his footsteps."

As the hooter sounded, Benny tossed the bread-wrapper from him and went back to the machine where Maisie Lynch was already getting into her stride for the afternoon, announcing that the only hope for a solution in Northern Ireland lay in three weeks non-stop prayer, prayer morning noon and night.

"Prayer will out," she said authoritatively. "Don't say I didn't tell you."

He finished up early that evening and went for a drink in the Turnpike Inn. Through the doorway of the extension a number of cardplaying factory men greeted him. The huge video was playing a blue movie, the men rigid as statues beneath interlocking bodies. In the corner pool balls clacked. Somewhere else a television blared. A fruit machine choked on coins. Benny was on his second drink when the northman came in and joined him at the bar. They knew one another well and stayed drinking together until closing time.

They did not broach the subject of the previous night until they were safely home in the northman's house on one of the council estates that had been recently built to accomodate the influx of norther-ners. His wife brought them tea and sandwiches. The northman tapped his thumbs and looked at Benny.

"They've been operating on this side of the border for over a year. It was them shot McCarney."

McCarney was the man whose body had been found dumped, shot through the head.

"They snatched him and took him across. It's the same outfit. UVF—the army are helping them."

Benny nodded.

"But they couldn't get across with the gear. They're picking them up this side."

"You're sure?" said Benny.

The northman nodded. "They have to be." He sipped his tea. "Somewhere near where it happened last night."

Outside a car passed, throwing shadows on the wallpaper.

"There's someone from the town helping them."

Benny shifted uneasily. The northman drew his breath and thought long and hard before he said, "We think we know who it is."

"Who?" said Benny sharply.

"I can't say. Not yet. I'll fill you in for definite tomorrow. He's being checked out. They're nearly a hundred per cent. He's known from a long time back." He paused. "The pigs this side won't touch them. They can do what they like. But it has to be stopped. McCarney was a good man. They nearly finished Quigley last night."

"Yes."

"We're going to need local men. We'll need back up."

"Yes."

"If you're needed . . . you might not be . . . can I rely on you?"

Benny replied, "Yes."

"Good," said the northman. "I'll talk to you when I know more. But we'll be moving soon."

They finished their tea and Benny set off for home. As he climbed the stairs, Tara cried out in her sleep. He hesitated on the landing and then, satisfied that all was well, crept in beside Sadie, but did not sleep until the first light of dawn was touching the frosted window.

XII

On her way to the Railway Hotel, Josie called at Abbeyville Gardens with a present for Tara and Darren Dolan. She stood on the doorstep with the neatly-wrapped package, reddening slightly as Sadie appeared, both children clinging on to her. Josie held out the present. "Come in," said Sadie. "Really Josie, you shouldn't have . . ."

They sat in the kitchen and had tea and scones. The children squealed excitedly as they wound up the clockwork toy. Both women avoided eye contact and did not stray from safe subjects. "The north is gone mad altogether," said Sadie tapping her cup handle. Josie nodded. They spoke of Christmas and increasing commercialisation. At one stage Sadie became so nervous because of the tension between them she almost blurted out, "It's her Josie. She doesn't want you here. But to hell with her. I'd love you to come. You were such a help to me before."

But she didn't. They just sat there listening to the tick of the clock and watching the snow advance and retreat outside. Then Josie rose and said, "I just thought I'd come and wish you all a Happy Christmas."

Sadie felt her stomach heave. She thought of Josie alone in the cottage on Christmas day, of how much she liked the kids and pleaded silently with herself to ask her to spend the Christmas with them but Mrs Dolan kept coming into her mind. *If I had known who she was in the first place she'd never have got in that door the like of her minding my grandchildren the house to herself God knows what could have happened to them God forbid but she could have killed those children Sadie she could have killed those children don't ever let her into this house again for if you do you'll never see me about the place again* . . .

"Well good luck now Sadie—and wish Benny all the best for me, won't you," said Josie.

Sadie helped her on with her coat and said goodbye. She stood in the doorway and waved as Josie turned the corner . . . *Kill those children how would she kill them you stupid bitch or have you any heart at all. Have you? Have you?*

But that was no good now.

The glass door of the Railway Hotel swung open before Josie and a scarf of cigarette smoke wrapped itself around her neck as she walked into the bar. She removed her wet overcoat and hung it up by the door. The barman spread his hands on the counter and winked, "The usual?"

Josie took the vodka and lime. She felt drowsy, the effect of the librium she had taken an hour before. The meeting with Sadie had depressed her. She drank the vodka in one gulp. The barman refilled it without being asked.

A snake of tinsel curled itself around the trade-marked mirror. Inside the oval of a Christmas card, a top-hatted city gent with a cane walked his dog through deep London snow. Santa Claus grinned broadly. On the television, a newsreader's deadpan voice announced, *A two hundred pound bomb exploded last night in the Catholic Ardoyne district of Belfast. Two people have been killed and five injured, three seriously. The Archbishop of Armagh has condemned the bombing, describing it as an outrage and an abomination . . ."* The eyes of the younger men at the bar narrowed as they listened. Then they looked away to put it out of their minds. The barman shook his head wearily, perplexed by it all. He leaned over to Josie and put his hand on her forearm. He winked again and whispered into her ear, "They'd be better off enjoying themselves. Eh Josie?" He looked into her eyes. He squeezed her arm again and went off laughing. Josie's lips were dry and her eyes heavy. She drank another vodka. A distraught woman described the scene of the bombing. Bodies everywhere, she said. She tried to steady her voice as the words stumbled out, *blinding flash, a loud bang, couldn't see anything. Bodies everywhere*, she repeated, *whoever did this must be sick that's all I can say*, she said as she broke down again and shielded her face with her hands.

The scene came into Josie's mind.

Bodies everywhere.

The ambulance with its blue light turning, white-faced policemen hauling away bodies in zippered bags. The two words would not go from her mind. *Bodies everywhere*. Bodies from the past.

The cleaning woman from the Bunch of Grapes who had died in the old folks home with no one near her. A shrivelled frame in a grey mortuary, hands crossed staring at the ceiling. Jack the Lad, the Northumbrian who often bought her drink, fading away in a bright airy hospital ward. A discarded suit of skin wept over by red-eyed relatives. A twitching body on Kilburn High Road, stunned companions screaming, "How did it happen? We were only coming out of the pub—the lights were green . . ." Time standing still as the passers-by watched the life ebb from him, a claw of blood on the side of his face, lips quivering like a helpless infant.

Cassie too, from far away in the days of her childhood, laid out by neighbour women who spoke in hushed tones of the best woman who ever lived. They folded her clothes lovingly and touched their lips with rosaries as they stared down at the padded coffin and said, "If there's one sure thing Cassie Keenan is walking the roads of the next world this night. She well and truly deserves her reward in the beyond." Cassie Keenan too had left her bones and skin behind her on a settle bed and had taken her leave to a place where what she was due would be paid in full.

Standing on a road that wound onward into a blueness that had no end, she smiled at Josie with a face that knew no care or distress and said, *If only you were here with me, my wee Josie, it would be like it was all those days ago. You and me as one. Look at the sky. See how warm and clear it is. Did you ever see fields so green Josie pet?*

Josie's throat went dry and she ordered another drink. She looked away from the sweat prints on the side of the glass. *When you come here you will be truly happy Josie. None of it will matter then. It will all be over.*

The nausea rising within her threatened to bring on a physical sickness. Josie clutched her glass. The barman was talking to her but all she could see was the movement of his lips and the contortions of his face. He filled her glass again. Smoke billowed to the ceiling. She was only vaguely aware of the presence beside her. The barman said, "Do you know Mr Murphy Josie?"

She looked at the red-knuckled hands on the counter, the nicotine-stained fingers. She shook her head.

"Ah, but I know you," said the heavily-built man. "At least I knew your father. The Buyer Keenan. Of course he was known high up and low down. Wasn't a road in Ireland that the Buyer Keenan didn't know." He placed his thumbs in his lapels and said to the barman. "That's a fact. The Buyer Keenan knew every road in this country. Anybody will tell you that. I'll have to buy his daughter a drink now, won't I? Fill them up again."

Josie drank the drinks as they were set before her. He sucked the wet tip of his cigarette and talked incessantly but Josie heard little of what he said. The music in the lounge came to an end and they stood for the national anthem. Josie took a last cigarette from the man and then stumbled to the door to get her coat. "Are you off Josie?" called the barman. "Are you not going to say goodnight to us?" She heard the tail-end of his laughter as she went out into the night. She went to the café and ate among the latenight adolescents and drunk farmers. She did not leave until well after one.

A policeman with a torch stood at the corner, the static spurting suddenly from the two-way radio by his side. Youths loitered, a discarded cigarette sailing across the street like a firework. Cars slowed as the policeman scrutinised the interiors, then revved up and sped off towards the border. Josie set off in the direction of the railway. The policeman looked after her, tapping his foot. The railway was littered with potholes. Passing the warehouses, Josie heard her name called. At first she thought it was her imagination and quickened her pace without turning around. Then she heard footsteps behind her. She turned suddenly to see the barman signalling, the other man behind him in the warehouse doorway.

"Josie," called the barman, "what do you say we have a bit of a party in your house? Just a couple of us, eh?"

Josie tensed and tried to steady the tremour in her voice. "No—I can't. Not in my house. I have to go." She turned from them.

"Why not? What's wrong with us? Is there something wrong with us? There was nothing wrong with our drink earlier on, eh? Just a couple of hours. We could have a good time. Come on Josie . . ."

She began to run. *Please Jesus please for Christ's sake*, she repeated. In the distance she heard her name called over and over. Then, carried off by the wind, she heard, "Go on then—you fucking ride!"

She stumbled twice on the twisted tracks before she reached the cottage.

Her heart was pounding in her chest. She closed the door behind her and barred it. Sweat broke out on her forehead. With trembling hands she lit the gas heater. She took off her wet clothes and left them to dry. The scarlet lamp burned and the Sacred Heart smiled. She pulled on a dressing gown and fell into the armchair. She shivered as the barman's voice echoed. She drifted in and out of sleep. The lamp twinged. *That'll be your father home from the market now, daughter,* her mother's voice whispered, *get on up the stairs and pray to Our Lady. Do you know what I'm going to tell you now Mrs Keenan? That husband of yours is known the length and breadth of Ireland. High up and low down, they know the Buyer Keenan. The Buyer is a well-respected man.*

She heard their voices as she stood among them all those years ago, their huge red hands dangling in front of her eyes as the Buyer stood at the bar, his stomach thrust out as he boasted, *No man in this town would ever best me. The Buyer's the roughest man in this town.*

She lay there for an hour and then there was a gentle tap on the door. She pulled the dressing gown about her and said, "Who is it?"

There was a long pause. "It's me . . . Pat."

Josie loosened. She went to the door and opened it. He looked away from her, his lank hair falling about his face. She took him inside to the dry warmth of the kitchen. He sat on the sofa, his eyes downcast. She spoke softly to him. He looked slowly upwards as if expecting to confront his executioner. She sat beside him and dried his hair briskly with a towel. When she was done, they went to the bedroom. He ranted breathlessly with his eyes closed about the priest and how he should have stood up to him. "But I can't Josie—it's as if they'll find out my secret if I stand up to them. I didn't want to do what the priest asked me. I don't believe in it. He talked me into it. I'm fifty years of age, Josie. I'm a hypocrite and a liar. I get sick to my stomach when I think about it. I'm ashamed Josie, ashamed, ashamed . . ."

When it was over and she had done what he wanted, she stroked his face and he blubbered to God how sorry he was about it all but Josie, he said, you like me don't you, you don't think I'm disgusting do you Josie do you . . ."

His arm fell limp and he began to wheeze in a fragile sleep punctuated with sudden uneasy cries. The protection of the drink and the drugs was beginning to wear off. Josie became agitated. *The length and breadth of Ireland,* the voice said to her again. But this time she felt the hard leathery rasp of her father's hand on her cheek and the smell of porter came into her nostrils. Stiff as a board she looked up at his bloodshot eyes as he stroked her hair with trembling hands.

Not a woman about this place since our Cassie died, wee pet. It's gone to rack and ruin. If only there was a woman would come in to see after you and me. There's no skin on God's sweet earth like the skin of a woman. Jesus like the skin of a woman. And as he quivered on top of Josie's body, outside the window the sun rose and Cassie was far away and would never come again, he cried bitterly as his body jerked, *I treated her bad. I treated our Cassie bad and I'll be damned in hell for it I should never have laid a finger on you my darling wee Josie.*

Cassie stood beneath the blue of the sky and smiled down the length of the winding road at Josie Keenan. She beckoned to her. But he was not there. The Buyer Keenan was nowhere to be seen. His cries came to her and the words again *bodies bodies*.

His face was not the face of the Buyer Keenan as she knew him. It was old and cracked and from his mouth issued a sort of howl as he cried, *The Buyer Keenan known the length and breadth of Ireland what happened to me where are the two women I loved?*

And on that grey road were random bones and littered skulls and as he stared up helplessly at the red sky above him and the burnt grasses that stretched as far as the eye could see, the buyer Keenan knew there was nobody now but himself. Through his tears he cried a terrified laughter and fell on his knees, the sound of his voice carrying for miles beyond. *You don't know me do you I'm the Buyer Keenan they all know me here like the length and breadth of Ireland I know it if you want to know the way to this place just keep walking till you're dead and take the first right for Paradise ha ha ha ha ha ha . . . but you'll find no Cassie here, poor Cassie's a long way from here . . . and me and her will never meet again . . .*

Josie tried to fight the tears coming to her eyes. It did no good, she told herself. She rose but she could not shake off the touch of Cassie's hand on her cheek as she said, "What if it had happened another way pet—who are we to know?"

Josie sat by the window but, brittle now after the flight of her protection, she could not halt any of it as it came at her. A small skeleton in the ground, a boy with a soft face, Culligan taking her hand as they sauntered through the streets of Dublin marvelling at the flocks of pigeons clustering around the statues of patriots. The Buyer taking her smiling through the coloured waves of people in the huge department stores.

There is no other way for me now, thought Josie, *there is only one way I can win now. I said I'd do it before and I will do it I will.*

Her hands were shaking as she took the tube of tablets from the shelf and emptied a handful of them into her mouth. She left the door open behind her and went out into the snow. She walked until she came to the bank of the lake. She stood there and brought all the voices back to her mind. She slowly waded into the water and hoped she'd faint. Three times she immersed herself but each time it became more difficult and when she saw herself as one of the bodies, with white bulging cheeks and a bloated stomach floating through the semi-opaque water, the fear took complete control of her. She could not break the surface the fourth time. She cried helplessly as she struggled back to the bank. She felt the strength going from her legs.

When she awoke it was dark again and the cramps tore at her stomach. A water hen skitted in the reeds.

The white fields stretched into the distance where a churchbell rang.

When she got back to the house, the gas fire had burnt itself out. Pat Lacey had gone, the bedclothes still in disarray. Josie clutched at the door to steady herself. When she saw the three twenty pound notes under the saucer she felt nothing. She just stood there staring into space, her wet nightdress flapping at her heels.

Far off in the town she heard the first rumblings of what she took to be thunder.

XIII

The explosion rocked the town.

The fire engine raced up and down the main street as if it had lost its way. The waitress in the Railway Hotel was hysterical, screaming help me help me. The siren skirled out into the night. The Christmas tree had toppled over and crashed through the Hypermarket window. The tarmac had cracked open and a burst watermain sent up a fountain of water like a huge orchid. A policeman in oilskins called nervously through a loudhailer, "Please go to your homes. There is no need to panic." But the more he appealed, the more people appeared in doorways, wandering through the streets in a daze. It was as if the place had fallen victim to an eerie mass hypnosis. They stared at the cables which criss-crossed the street with glazed eyes. The policeman became frantic and cried out, "Will you please go home! Those cables are live!"

But nobody listened to him. A plume of smoke went up over the Vintage Bar. Flames licked at the tangled mass of metal, the tyres melting on to the kerb. The water from the burst main swirled into the gutters. "There may be more devices," called the policeman. "Please go to your homes." A rafter tumbled and a window caved in. Slates fell from the roofs and frightened dogs howled.

Eventually police reinforcements began to arrive. Water hoses stretched the length of the street. The police ushered the dumbstruck people away and lined the kerbs with no-parking buoys. They cordoned off the area and stood straddle-legged at each end clutching two-way radios. The waitress in the hotel was taken away with a number of others in an ambulance. Rumours bred and run amok. A child in a bedroom in the house opposite the pub had been blinded. The chief of staff of the IRA had been in the bar. A farmer had lost his legs. Nobody knew what to believe. The crumpled wreck of the Austin 1100 was towed away. Volunteers began to sweep away the water and debris. The shattered clockface of the church looked down forlornly at the chaos on The Diamond. Stretcher bearers waited anxiously at the town hall praying there would be no work for them to do. Families checked the recent movements of their own and made frantic phone calls. The firemen went to work on the interior of the Vintage Bar. It was not long before they found the first body. Word shot through the streets like wildfire. Who was it who was it, they asked, someone local, was it was it? The face was blackened with smoke and the body charred but it did not take the fireman long to identify the dead body.

It was Joe Noonan.

The other man was a stranger.

The only other casualty was the barman who had escaped with minor injuries and was now in a neighbour's house in shock.

The people of the town shook their heads in disbelief when they heard. They stared out of their windows trying to make sense of it all. The labourers prepared themselves for a busy night as the clip of hammers rang out and the blackened façades were boarded up. Signs were placed at either end of the street. DANGER—STAY AWAY.

The water orchid shrunk and the firemen rolled up their hoses.

Patrol cars cruised the whole night long.

In the days that followed, the town filled up with journalists and visiting politicans. They packed the hotel and interviewed many of the locals. Joe Noonan was described as "one of the nicest lads about the town". Pat Lacey appeared on national television and spoke of "the perpetrators of this dastardly deed". It became a sort of jamboree as everyone scanned the screen hoping for a glimpse of themselves or their house.

Then out of nowhere, it all stopped. The microphone wires were gathered up, the suitcases packed and, almost immediately, it was as if they had never been there. The lounge of the Railway Hotel emptied and the waitress was back on duty as usual. The patrol cars became less frequent. The crack in the main street was filled in and the clockface repaired. The locals slowly went back to their ordinary lives as if they were emerging from a drug-induced trance. The proprietor of the Vintage Bar nailed up a notice *Business As Usual* on the door.

At Mass, the priest gave out the details of Joe Noonan's funeral. As the dust settled, the people of the town tried to get the incident into perspective. The question that burned in their minds was, "Who had done it?"

Certainly not the IRA who were hardly going to bomb the town where fifty years before Matt Dolan had led the raid on the railway and put Carn in the history books as a republican and nationalist town. The debate raged and new theories were advanced by the day but it all came to an abrupt end when, in a phonecall to a Belfast newspaper, a protestant para-military organisation claimed responsibility for the action and said that there would be repeats if the supporters of the IRA in such towns did not withdraw their support for the campaign of genocide against the protestant people along the border.

At first the reaction to this was one of fury and indignation. It brought out the worst in many, who said that if that was their attitude, they deserved all they got. Vengeful plots against protestants living in the area were spoken of but none were taken really seriously and evaporated almost as soon as they were mentioned. They swore that they would not be frightened and intimidated by these thugs, that they had a right to walk the streets of their own town without fearing for their own safety. But as time went by and they thought more deeply about it, the more anxious they became.

What if there was a repetition? They might not be

so lucky next time. Carn was a small town. What if the bomb was even bigger next time? Any of them could wind up like Joe Noonan, hauled away in a zippered bag. They thought of their children lying dead beneath blackened masonry, trapped in burning cars.

For the first time it dawned on them that they were no longer talking about pictures in history books and images on a television screen.

Then the local politician went on the radio and said that the blame for the bomb could be laid fairly and squarely at the door, not of the protestant people, who were a decent and God-fearing people, but of everyone in Ireland, both north and south, who had ever promoted violence or turned a blind eye to it. He said that we should never forget that nearly a million people in the fourth green field did not see themselves as invaders or strangers at all. The architects of the terrible deed were in fact the Provisional IRA and their supporters. It was they who should be reviled and cast out from the community. It was these agents of the devil who, indirectly, had bombed Carn.

This speech seemed to have a tremendous impact in the town. The politician was a well-respected man. When arms were found in a disused farmhouse outside the town and more police and military were drafted in, the people began to whisper that the town had seen enough trouble. They averted their eyes when the trucks rattled up and down the main street. They did not want to be implicated and did not want their town blown up again. They sought refuge now in a feigned naivity. "What's it all about anyway?" they said, in the hope that a new found innocence would reduce the chances of violence returning to their streets.

When Francie Mohan was arrested and beaten up in the police station for singing a republican song in the Turnpike Inn, they took no notice of it and said that, knowing Francie, there was probably two sides to it, he had probably assaulted the policeman.

A committee which had been formed before to plan the next year's Easter Commemorations quietly disbanded itself. They stored the tricoloured flags and bundles of proclamations of independence in a back room in the town hall and wrote to the various politicians who came every year saying that they would no longer be required to speak in Carn at Easter, that it was thought to be "indiscreet" to hold the commemoration this year.

Whenever Matt Dolan's raid on the railway came up accidentally in casual conversation, or was alluded to by a stranger, they cut the discussion short by saying, "That was a long time ago."

And when Francie Mohan drunkenly shouted the speeches of Patrick Pearse and Wolfe Tone across The Diamond every Saturday night, they steeled themselves and tried not to hear but when it became too much for them they turned and looked away redfaced, as if he were some kind of imbecilic relative who had turned up out of nowhere at an important family wedding.

Benny had called at the Noonan house as soon as he heard the news. Joe's sister, inconsolable, had told him how her brother had driven herself and the kids to Dublin for the day and on the way home had gone in for a drink while he waited for them to get chips in the Yankee Doodle. Her face was red-raw as she said over and over again, "It was me asked him to wait, Benny. What will we do without him? I loved our Joe so much, Benny."

Benny stayed with the family the whole night, reliving parts of Joe's life as if they felt that enough emotional intensity on their part would somehow bring him back.

When Benny felt his own tears coming, he went to the bathroom and stayed there for over an hour. By the time the gentle tap came at the door, the sorrow in him had passed and in its place there was bitterness and anger, deeper than any he had ever imagined he could contain within himself.

XIV

The mourners stood on the hill overlooking the town. The surplice flapped in the priest's face as he struggled with pages of the missal. The drone was carried off by the wind. Joe's sister broke down and threw herself on the coffin crying bastards the bastards, her mantilla falling from her face. The priest averted his eyes compassionately. They lowered the box into the ground and she clutched Benny's arm. The fistful of clay tumbled on the wood and a lively babble began as they slowly drifted towards the gate of the cemetery. They went to the Vintage Bar which still bore traces of the explosion. Faded black streaks scored the ceiling and there was a shattered wall lamp in the corner. They began to drink frenziedly as if they feared they were now about to go the way of Joe Noonan. Benny and Sadie sat together out of the way. Clichés were exchanged with vigour. So young. We never know. Cut down in his prime. The Good Lord does His harvesting and He leaves none behind. Benny felt as if he were floating over their heads. The whole town seemed to be in the pub.

Many of them made their way over awkwardly to them and pumped Benny's hand, bleary-eyed. They shook their heads and looked away as if they had forgotten how to speak. Others leaned over and whispered furtively, "I know you and him felt the same way. It's time this business in the north was sorted out once and for all."

Eventually as the drink went in, they forgot about Benny Dolan. Then they more or less forgot about Joe Noonan. Sadie leaned over and said morosely, "Sometimes you'd wonder Benny. It's not much of a way to remember anyone, is it?"

The floor was littered with cigarette ends and broken glass. An argument over a long forgotten football match rose above the din and others lent their voices to the fray. Racing blared out. "One hundred and eighty," shouted a darts player. Sadie stroked the back of Benny's hand absentmindedly. The notion of someone as vivacious as Joe Noonan lying dead in a wooden box just wouldn't make itself real to her. She felt nothing, only guilt for feeling nothing.

Coming towards closing time, they began to congregate about Benny once more as if they felt he was the most authentic representative of the dead man. "The bikes," they said to him. "You and Joe and the bikes. The two of you were wild in those days, eh?"

After a while Benny heard nothing.

Outside in the street Sadie said, "Well that's that. That's it all over. Rotten, isn't it?"

"What can you do?" replied Benny. "Unless it's

their own nobody gives a fuck. That's the long and the short of it."

They got into the car and drove off in the direction of Abbeyville Gardens. They turned into the driveway to see a neighbour standing under their porch lamp. She signalled to them anxiously. Sadie ran over to her. There was a crumpled body lying at her feet.

"She's been lying there all evening," said the neighbour, distraught. "I've been keeping watch on her. She just lay down there. I didn't know whether to call the police or what. I didn't know who she was. The children were all around her. I mean, it's not good for them is it? She was ranting and raving to herself. I think she's been drinking all day."

The woman shook her head, mystified. "I don't know what the world is coming to," she said. "The like of that." She turned on her heel and crossed the road to her own house. Other doors quietly closed.

"Give me a hand Benny," said Sadie.

They took Josie in and laid her on the sofa. Sadie dabbed her forehead with a cold towel. There was a slight gash on her cheek where she had fallen. Every so often unintelligible phrases issued from her lips. She made sudden jerky movements in her sleep. They waited with her for over two hours. Then her eyes opened and she cried out, perplexed by her surroundings, "Don't touch me! Don't touch me!"

Sadie touched her gently on the arm. She was sweating.

"Sadie . . . you're here. I called up but you weren't here . . ."

"It's okay. It's okay now Josie."

Benny said, "I'll make some hot coffee Josie. That's what you need."

Josie looked helplessly at Sadie. "I just wanted to talk Sadie. I know you've a lot on your plate. I'm worried Sadie. I'm afraid I'll do something to myself. I'm not able to sleep, things keep coming back to me, things I should have left behind long ago. Half the time, my mind's not my own. It scares me Sadie. I've nobody now. I needed to talk to someone."

The older woman's breathing was tense. She picked at her nail as the continued. "I can't stay out in that house much longer. I lie there most of the night staring at the ceiling, waiting for more terrible things to come into my head. I'm afraid Sadie, that's the truth. I'll have to get out of this town. I'll have to go back to England. I can't stay here. I can't stay out in that cottage much longer. Things turned out bad for me Sadie."

Sadie clasped her hand tightly. "Josie," she said. "It should never have happened the way it did. You should never have stopped coming up here. It was my fault. I let it happen. Josie—promise me you'll come up soon. Never mind what happened. Never mind any of it. It will never happen again. You can be sure of that. Will you?"

Josie smiled. "People are people Sadie. You can't change them." She squeezed Sadie's hand. "It's good of you to listen to me Sadie. It takes my mind off things to talk. There's too much in my mind."

She chewed at her underlip. "Sadie?" she said.

"Yes."

"If ever anything happened—would you see to my funeral?"

"Josie for God's sake . . ."

"I have nobody else Sadie . . . would you?"

"Of course I would, you don't have to . . ."

Benny arrived back with the coffee.

They went back to the first day they had all met at Una Lacey's wedding, the subsequent chance meetings in the hotel and the evenings babysitting.

"The town will never be the same without young Noonan," said Josie.

Benny lapsed into long periods of silence when his name came up.

Sadie and Josie sat talking for over two hours.

Josie came back from the bathroom and thanked Sadie again. She donned the borrowed coat and hesitated in the doorway.

"Call up tomorrow Josie if you're feeling up to it."

"Thanks Sadie," said Josie.

Benny revved the car engine and Josie slipped into the passenger seat. He waved and sped off towards the railway. The Hairy Mountains reared up and out of the darkness. When they got to the cottage, Josie reached in her handbag and pressed a ten pound note into Benny's hand. Benny pushed it away. She thanked him again, and brushing her hair back from her eyes got out of the car and set off across the overgrown railway track. Benny kept the engine running and looked after her to make sure she made it to the small cottage nestled in the crook of two drumlins. He stared at the blunt outline of the railway building, moss-whiskered and covered with weeds. The engine sheds had caved in on themselves, a wreckage of twisted girders and broken concrete. He remembered it as it had once been, the locomotives puffing in and out of the town the whole day long, endless traffic to and from the now derelict building. He scanned the field again. A light burned in the window of the cottage. He cleaned the windscreen with a chamois, the snow was beginning again. He sighed and his head fell on the steering wheel. The voice went through his head.

"That cunt Cooney has the back worked off me. Come on for a pint."

Someone helping them this side, the northman's voice said. Has to be. Has to be.

The dawn was breaking over the town by the time he got back.

The Golden Book of the Sacred Heart, said Cassie. Do you know Josie wee pet you can have any name enrolled in this book and you can have a young man educated to the priesthood and sent far and wide across the globe to preach the faith of our fathers to those less fortunate. Cassie smiled and stroked the imitation leather cover as if it were a living

thing. She turned the pages gently and her voice was music to Josie's ears. Josie looked up and saw that the book was bathed in a golden light and the inscribed names of all the holy people in Carn swarmed out from it like the souls in purgatory to fill the room. Mr Peter Cassidy Miss Eileen Kelly The Reilly Family. Oh look, cried Cassie, look at that Josie, that's your own your very own name in the copperplate handwriting of Canon Martin himself. Look Miss Josephine Keenan just under my own Kathleen Keenan and William Keenan. Your very own name in the holy book.

Oh hello Josie, I saw your name in the Golden Book and your own lad how is he? He must be a fair age by now. The last time I saw him he was eight years old, you were off to Dublin in Mooney's minibus. Yes we went, just me and him I took him to the top of Nelson's Pillar and then we went to the Savoy for an ice-cream. It was one of the best days we ever had. He's a good boy and doing well at his school. What did you say his name was Josie? Vincent, little Vincent, that's his name, Josie Culligan.

Annie Lennon.

Josie Culligan.

Mrs James McDonald.

Marion McCabe.

Josie Culligan.

Margaret Malone.

Josie?

The names were chanted in a distant chapel.

Michael McCaffrey.

Edward Maguire.

Seamus Smith.

The McMahons.

Are you in there Josie? Open the door.

Des McCarron.

Mary Ann McDonagh.

JJ Egan.

The Martins.

Josie let me in or I'll drop with the cold.

Josie awoke in sheets drenched with sweat. The Sacred Heart lamp flame waltzed on the wall in front of her. She pasted back her hair and tried to shake her thoughts away. The voice came again and her whole body stiffened.

For the love of God Josie, let me in.

She could not place the voice and went cold all over. Fragments of imagination and reality came at her from different directions. She fumbled her way to the kitchen and took down the librium from the shelf. She emptied a few down her throat. She could see a shadow on the curtain. She tried to pour water into a cup but she couldn't manage it. She waited for the drug to draw its comforting silk around her mind but she was too taut, her body fighting against it.

She felt for the latch on the door. The barman from the hotel stood facing her with a brown paper bag under his arm. Behind him, looking away from her was the heavily built man, Jack Murphy. She could see that their eyes were bloodshot with drink.

"What do you want?" she said.

The barman grinned. "Lord bless us Josie, I thought you were never going to open the door. What do we want?"

He held up the bag. "We brought you a little drink. On account of it being the festive season and that ..."

"You can't come in here . . . please . . . it's too late . . ."

But the barman had already eased his way past her and was standing in the centre of the kitchen. He surveyed his surroundings. "The Sacred Heart, eh? Good to see that you have the man above on the wall to mind you. Not that you'd need minding from me and Jack, seeing as we know one another so well. Come on in out of the cold Jack, you'll get your death."

Jack Murphy came in and closed the door behind him. He stood beneath the Sacred Heart.

The barman rubbed his hands. "Now," he said, "What about an opener?"

"I haven't got an opener," Josie said.

The barman raised his eyebrows in mock horror. "No opener? How can we have a party with no opener? Josie—I'm suprised at you." He took the bottle from the bag and bit the cap off with his teeth. He spat it into the fireplace. "What do we need an opener for anyway? Eh Josie?"

He drank from the bottle. Then he moved towards Josie. He held it out to her. "Here you are now. Have a drop."

Josie turned away.

"What's wrong with you? Not want a drop, do you not? You weren't so quick to refuse drink in the hotel. You were keen enough then, weren't you?"

He drank again. "'Course you're keen on a lot of things when it suits you."

Josie said nothing.

The barman laughed. "Look at her Jack," he cried, waving the bottle, "you'd think she was the Little

Flower standing there hiding herself. You'd think it was the fucking Little Flower herself Jack."

Jack Murphy didn't reply, fidgeting nervously and looking towards the window.

"What do you think we are—imbeciles? You think I'm some sort of half-wit that doesn't know what goes on? I've been watching you a long time now Keenan, I've been watching you too long not to know what game you're playing. You think I've nothing better to do than fill your glass and wipe up after you? Think I've nothing better to do than fill you up with drink? Eh?"

He passed the bottle to the other man, "Oh, me and Jack here heard a few home truths about you. From an old friend of yours."

He stood over Josie. "A friend of yours this long time."

He took her chin in his hand and tilted her face forward. "Mr Lacey. Aye, that's right, Pat. Me and Jack know Pat well."

He held her in a vicegrip. "What does Pat like?"

He pulled her towards him and his tongue darted into her mouth. "I don't have to ask you that you know. He told us." He burst out laughing. "The bollocks let it all out. Gave it all out after a skinful of whiskey after hours in the Railway."

He wiped the tears from his eyes and said, "I thought a woman like you would have more sense than to have truck with a blabbermouth. You're his mammy, are you? Mrs Lacey, eh?" He sneered.

"That's Lacey's game, eh? How could you go near a man like that? You'd have liked his wee speech in the back bar all right—muttering and slabbering like a child. I don't know what comes over me he says, God help me God forgive me she makes me want things a man should know nothing about. From the day and hour she set foot in this town I've never had rest. If the like of that ever got out. Jack thinks you should leave poor Mr Lacey alone. Me, I don't give a fuck for Lacey."

He forced his tongue into her mouth again. "Now me—I wouldn't blab. You could be sure of that."

He gripped her tightly about the shoulders and forced her slowly to the floor. "I heard plenty of stories Josie. What about Vinnie Culligan, the fly boy butcher that robbed half the town and fucked off to England. I heard he left one or two things behind him."

He unzipped his flies and stood over her.

"What was it like in England Josie? Used to the high life were you?"

He pulled out his penis. "I'd say you seen plenty of these in England." He held it in his hand and stared down at her, whitefaced.

"Lacey's like this?" he said in a whisper. "Eh?"

He pushed her down and heaved himself on top of her. She cried out and he caught her by the throat. "Don't."

She scratched at his face and he squeezed her neck until she could barely breathe. He held her there and slowly withdrew his hand.

"Don't," he repeated. "Understand?"

"No ... for Christ's sake ..." pleaded Jack Murphy.

He pulled her dressing gown up over her waist and

drove it into her again and again. He groaned as if in terrible pain. His whole body shook as he spurted and withdrew haplessly. He stumbled backwards, a clown with his trousers about his knees and his braces dangling. His hands began to shake as he pulled up his trousers.

His eyes were filled with fear and hatred. "Now Keenan. Now I know what you're like. I know your game now, why you have to hurt him. That's all you can do Keenan, because you hate it, you've never liked it in your life. I've seen women like you. The Buyer was fond of the women too, wasn't he? Kept it in the family, didn't he? The rough tough Buyer, that was his style in the end too. Him and Lacey be well met. I'll tell you what, you stay out of my way in the future, you hear? Stay out of the Railway Hotel! And don't think of telling anybody about this if you're wise— not that they'd believe the likes of you anyway . . ."

"Come on . . . for the love of Jesus," cried Jack Murphy.

Stray flakes of snow blew into the kitchen as they went out into the morning.

She lay there on the floor for the whole day long. The snow came and went at the window, the day passed and the light began to fade. Josie tasted salt in her mouth. The cold sweat dried on her skin. *There you are now, a grand sight on your kitchen floor Miss Lollobrigida, it's a pity your doctor husband isn't here to help you now, what a shock he'd get if he were to walk in and see the cut of his sweet young bride.*

Josie cried and cried bitterly. The Sacred Heart became a grey silhouette. She felt her way to the bathroom. The side of her face was numb. A hag looked at her from the mirror and filled her with revulsion. Between her legs she felt him pushing again and again. His face came at her and she tried to release herself by going forward, by lunging at the image, watching herself killing him, blood pouring from the folds of his neck. She spat phlegm into the basin. The more she backed off from him, the more terror and pain she felt. She forced herself and his head went back and she did it to him over and over.

She did not sleep. Her body had her primed for an imminent disaster she could not name. Her fists would not unclench. Her breathing was tangled up in her chest. In the corner the stained dressing gown lay in a heap. When she looked at it out of the corner of her eye she began to cry again and her whole body shivered. She took a heavy cardigan from the cupboard and put it on. *Ah that's no outfit for La Lollo, the woman who stunned the streets of Manchester when she skipped off the bus all those years ago. You weren't always like this, make sure they know it, oh no, you had a face that could stop the street and no mistake, Phil Brady would vouch for that. You didn't get a doctor husband but you got Phil Brady and a few others. Didn't you Josie? You got a thirteen stone docker who liked to dress up for you. And a man from Mayo who cried like a baby in your arms. Not to mention Pat Lacey—Pat Lacey the important official! You did very well for yourself Josie—who cares about a doctor husband? Oh there's no doubt, you could have got what you wanted had the dice tumbled the other way. But sure then, who couldn't? Who couldn't Josie. The thing is, it didn't. Eh? It didn't Josie. That's the trouble, you have to take what you get. Look at Cassie. Look what she got. Did you want her life? You did, didn't you? All you ever wanted was to be her. All your life you wanted to be Cassie Keenan, the best woman that ever lived, and look what happened. Culligan put you on the wrong road and now you're in with nobody, even the Sacred Heart will turn His back on you after all your trickery. Pity you didn't stick it out like Cassie Josie. She's on the pig's back now in that blue and never-ending place and damn the bit of her you'll ever see, neither you nor the Buyer and his rough roving hands will ever set eyes on Cassie Keenan again.*

She held the dress in her hands. The camphor smell filled her nostrils. It was black satin, the dress she had worn the first day she walked into the Moss Side bar. It was a Gina Lollobrigida dress. Her hair bobbed and a string of pearls. In the room over the pub she spent hours posing. A whole week's wages gone on perfume. The swish of the net underskirt as she flitted behind the bar and watched their eyes as they strained for a glimpse of her legs. It would look good with the veins in her legs and the black marks the barman had left like a pretty little string of beads on her abdomen.

She sat at the window. The flesh of her arms bulged out through the tight-fitting sleeves. Her eyes were raw-red. A robin looked at her from the railway track and then went back to its foraging.

They all came together now in her mind. A room of whispers and half-heard guffaws. And who was there with them only Vinnie, still with the nicotine on his fingers and the broad smile on his fresh face. Him and Lacey and Murphy and the barman would have a lot to talk about now. They all knew Josie Keenan. They would be able to have a good long chat about her, no danger of silence in that company. With the whole room to themselves, not a woman in sight, no women to come between them and their clandestine talk of bodies, more bodies, dead or alive it was all the same to them.

Time went on. Josie's tears dried. Her face muscles loosened. But they did not go away. They all sat there and the drink went down and arms went around shoulders. They clasped one another and swore their secrecy. Vinnie looking well as ever with his hair brylcreemed and a gold pin in his tie that he must have got in England. The barman shaking his head as he began the story anew. But Pat stopped laughing. No, Pat wasn't the same as Vinnie. He wasn't the same as the barman and now it was coming out as they stared at him confusedly. He was talking daft and there were tears in his eyes too. "The bitch does things to me. I should never have gone near her. She makes me give her money. She's a bad woman and she lived in all the worst dens in England. I'm not like that men. I never wanted to do them things. I'm like you men. I'll never go near her again. I'm like any other man. I am! I swear! I say, you gave her what for, you and Jack gave her what for, eh?" He clutched the barman's arm and looked hungrily into his face. "I say you gave her a dose of her own medicine. That will put a stop to her gallop, eh?" He held his privates with his hand. "You gave her a rub of the relic, didn't you? That will settle the bitch's hash. You won't tell anyone about me, will you?"

Then Vinnie went, gathering himself up and off

with a smile. Then the barman went. Pat Lacey was left sitting in the room by himself, looking about him furtively with a drink in his hand as if expecting someone. He got up and went to the door. He was edgy. "Josie," he said, "you didn't hear me. You didn't take all that seriously did you? I was only having a bit of a laugh. A bit of a laugh with the boys . . . I never thought he'd go out to you Josie . . . Josie, please . . ."

All over Josie was like an open wound. She stared at him. The wisps of hair fell over his eyes like Phil Brady's years before. The same eyes as the barman as he groaned on top of her, siphoning his poison into her. Poison that coursed through her. She was stone cold as she stared at Pat Lacey. He moved back against the table. He didn't know which way to turn. Molloy shouted, *You'll thieve no more in this house* and the nun towered above her and gripped her wrist but Josie steadied herself and cried inside, *Not this time not this time do you hear me?*

Her head fell but there were no tears. Her fingers were purple with the cold. She lit the gas heater. In the glass a reflection distorted by tiny rivers of melted snow looked back at her, a jumbled mosaic. The dress was way above her knee. The room reeked of mothballs and stale perfume. A right looking sketch lads, eh, it'd take a good man to get up on the likes of that. What about the barman, I hear he'd get up on the crack of dawn ha ha ha ha. La Lollo, eh, is that what she calls herself, it's a wonder with all that money she couldn't get a dress to fit her. Maybe she should go back to Moss Side. Maybe there's hard-up lads there would go for her. Maybe there's hard-up lads there would be able to touch her with a barge pole. All she'll get about here is Lacey or the barman—*and he'd get up on the crack of dawn! I say he'd get up on the crack of dawn, boys!*

Her stomach heaved. She plucked at the sleeve of the dress. She searched for the smiling face of Cassie, listened for the soft voice calling her to that place. But there was nothing except the flap of the gas fire and the wind outside.

She went cold all over. It was different now. This time it was different. This time she had been asked to bear too much.

"This time it's different. Not this time," the words went through her mind. "This time it's different. This time it's different."

Lacey.

XV

James Cooney had come up with the goods again. The week after the bomb an envelope containing a cheque for eight hundred pounds had landed on Pat Lacey's desk. It was from James Cooney and was made payable to the "Bomb Damage Appeal".

JR Ewing could go and take a run and jump at himself. He simply wasn't in the same league as the owner of the Carn Meat Processing Plant. That was the view of the workers on the factory floor and there weren't many in the town who would argue with it.

Who could begrudge a man like that his mansion? Wasn't he entitled to it? He had worked damned hard to get it, harder than JR Ewing or any of his ilk. And he had spent his money at home into the bargain. The money he had donated to the Bomb Damage Appeal simply showed that there was no end to the man's good nature.

As one worker put it, in Carn, James Cooney was still "A1".

So when the shop steward announced in the canteen that the entire workforce were to be addressed by Mr Cooney himself, the air tingled with excitement. Hot on the heels of his generous donation to the council, what new goodies was he going to come up with? He was going to give them a really good Christmas present to bring home to their wives. He had something good up his sleeve for his workers and he wanted to spring it on them as a surprise. Word travelled through the factory that it was to be a triple bonus for every man. Conversation hummed after the break as they waited for the hooter to call them to the canteen for this great announcement. That was the great thing about James Cooney, that was what made him better than all the factory owners put together— he was always ten steps ahead of the posse. Nobody could ever pinpoint exactly what was going on in his head. The workers wound themselves up like coiled springs debating the nature of the surprise. Whatever it was to be, they saw before them pay packets bulging like never before. It was like waiting for Santa Claus. They pestered the shop stewards and the union officials to give them more information but they just waved them away and said that they had been told to say nothing. All they knew was that Mr Cooney wanted to talk personally to the men. Beyond that their lips were sealed.

As the sides of beef whirred past and the giblets were sealed inside plastic bags, children's bicycles were bought, new televisions rented, wives' faces lit up and gleaming hi-fis beamed from living room corners. The afternoon stretched like eternity. But eventually the hooter went, aprons were thrown off and every man made his way to the canteen atremble with anticipation.

James Cooney was looking snappier than usual. He wore a three-piece pinstripe suit and a starched white shirt. The Production Manager and two union officials sat behind him at a table with notes and a clipboard in front of them. The Production Manager toyed with a silver fountain pen as he watched the men file in. There was a hubbub of chatter and smoke billowed to the ceiling. They pulled up chairs and settled themselves. Gradually the din began to die down. They leaned forward expectantly, full sure that James Cooney would begin his address with an anecdote or a funny story of some kind. But had they not been so excited by the fantasies which had taken root throughout the course of the afternoon, they would have noticed that James Cooney was wearing an expression which was far from lighthearted. He looked at his shoes and his brow was knit anxiously. At the table the union officials gave all their attention to their notes.

James Cooney cleared his throat and played with his gold watchstrap. Silence floated down on the assembly like a parachute. James Cooney paced up and down, then began to speak. He started on about his time in industry in America. How he had started off as a teaboy in a steel mill in Pennsylvania. How at one stage of his career he had had four jobs at once. Then he went on to his dreams. The greatest dream of all, he said, had always been to come back to the town of his birth. To give it all he had, to build it from the bottom up and make it the envy of every town in the country. He had wanted, from the day he left *The Shores of Erin* to come back and turn Carn into a boom town, a town that would never want for anything. A town that would forget forever the closing of the railway. A town that would never again helplessly watch its youth take the emigrant boat to England and New York.

From the day he had stepped off the steamer with his suitcase and his coat under his arm, he had dreamed of making it all come true. His arms spread out to embrace the buildings of the plant.

He spoke fondly of the first delivery of cattle by a local farmer. Men who had been with him at the very beginning and since moved on were wistfully recalled. *Believe me, men, those were glorious days. Glorious days.*

He went through the development and growth of the factory month by month, year by year.

As he went on, the workers began to shift about uncomfortably in their seats. They lit cigarettes and looked around them. They didn't like the way James Cooney was going on, This was not his usual form, going back over old times, raking over old dead coals that most of them had long since forgotten. He cared about the farmer who had delivered cattle on the first day? That was like the way the old people went on about the railway. Where was the joke, the anecdote and the way forward? That was what they wanted, to hell with the way back. They wanted to hear about the triple bonuses and the fat brown packages of bank-notes that were coming their way.

When he had finished on the subject of times past in the factory, he turned and smiled at the Production

Manager who came forward with the clipboard. He was an unpopular man, with none of the style of James Cooney. He was a no-nonsense, greyfaced man who shot off home in his Sierra every evening dead on six o'clock. Figures were his life. He talked figures non-stop and when the conversation was about some other subject, he could never rest until it had been switched to his favourite topic. Now he was in his element. James Cooney took a back seat as he went about his business in the same manner as the icy businessman from the Great Northern Railway had done years before. He looked the men straight in the eye as he unrolled a litany of figures which completely threw them, unprepared as they were for anything so sterile and demanding. What dislocated them even more was that James Cooney and the union officials seemed to have taken on expressions as grave and doom-laden as the speaker. They held their heads and tapped their chins gravely. When the words "realistic" and "serious changes" were used, James Cooney nodded morosely. The Production Manager outlined the reasons for the suddenness of the meeting. Mr Cooney had always believed in being straight. Everyone knew that. He did not believe in leading the workers up the garden path. They had talked long and hard about it. They knew that they could rely on the maturity of the men to face up to the facts and make difficult, unpalatable decisions. He spoke of a crisis in the cattle industry. Things had taken a disturbing turn for the worse in the past six months. Oil prices had hit every kind of production. Inflation was currently running at fifteen per cent and rising.

Then he put down the clipboard. His speech slowed and he gestured unnecessarily, as if explaining a problem to a dim child. He said that it now appeared that they had expanded too quickly. There was now a glut of beef in Europe. It was time for everyone to realise, and not just in the beef industry—he turned for a second to receive James Cooney's nod of approval—that the winds of change were blowing. The icy winds of change are blowing around this country and if we do not face up to this, we could be in serious trouble, he said. The good times were coming to an end. Then he fell silent and looked down the length of the canteen. They looked up at him with their mouths hanging open. Like the railway workers of years before, they half-expected him to suddenly fling the documents and clipboard papers from him and burst out laughing, crying, "I certainly had you fooled there, eh? I took you in there, lads? I took you all in hook line and sinker."

But he didn't. He went back once more to his documents and before they knew it they were again up to their necks in a welter of figures and numbers and percentages and dates and statistics. It seemed like it would never end.

When he had finished, James Cooney rose once more and said that it was one of the greatest regrets of his life that he had had to gather so many of the best workers it had ever been his privilege to employ together to break this sad news. But the current climate and forces outside his control had left him little choice. He truly appreciated everything the people of Carn had done for him. The like of the workers assembled here today are to be found nowhere in the British Isles, or anywhere else for that matter, he said.

It would be a sad day for Carn when the Carn Meat Processing Plant closed down in the new year.

When he spoke these words, the men felt themselves go cold. The words reverberated in their heads. *Were they dreaming or what? What was Cooney on about? Had he lost his mind—closed?*

No.

He was talking about the possibility—if the climate was right— of a temporary re-opening during the summer. But there was no way that could be guaranteed.

They would just have to wait and see.

Then the Production Manager announced that the redundancy terms would be negotiated properly and fairly with the unions. Then he began to gather up his papers and put them into his leather briefcase.

Slowly James Cooney's face began to come back to its old self. His eyes brightened and he smiled as he said that he had taken the liberty of organising a special Christmas party for every worker in the factory. It was to be a party to end them all, a token of his thanks to the town. And for the first two hours there will be a free bar, not one man will have to put his hand in his pocket, he said.

It was to take place in the Turnpike Inn the following evening.

Thank you for your time, he said and with a little wave, he was gone, followed by the Production Manager carrying his zippered briefcase.

As soon as he disappeared uproar broke out. Directionless sputniks flew everywhere as they cried, "What about the triple bonus? He can't do this to us! Where are the union men now? What about all the big promises?" The tone became frantic.

But they lost the run of themselves and any kind of meaning or sense was lost. On the way home, rumours bred and spread like a bushfire. They claimed that Cooney had never owned the factory, that he had merely been a front man for a conglomerate who had made a fortune out of EEC intervention and were now running for cover and keeping the spoils. They were dumping the workers now when it suited them. The more they talked, the more ludicrous the rumours became. They clenched their fists bitterly as they spoke his name. He had never been in America at all, they claimed. They did not go home but went straight to the public bars and hotels. They felt like infants abandoned in the wilderness. They stumbled homewards in the early hours of the morning shouting, "Cooney the liar" and "Cooney betrayed Carn. We were better off in the days of the railway."

And when at last the streets were empty, the barmen in the Turnpike Inn set up their ladders and unrolled the banner James Cooney had had specially printed a week before. They draped it across the façade and went across the street to admire it. In giant red and black letters it proclaimed to the citizens of Carn:

MEAT PLANT PARTY! JAMES COONEY WELCOMES YOU ALL TO THE TURNPIKE INN—FREE BAR FOR ALL EMPLOYEES FOR TWO HOURS—TURNPIKE INN CHRISTMAS BONANZA PARTY!

Be there!

XVI

The northman heaved the crate onto the truck and waited until the loading bay was deserted. The last of the nightshift workers drifted towards the exit. He looked about him and lit a cigarette. Then he sat down. Below them the sprawling town slept. The northman sighed and dragged on the cigarette. "So, here we are Benny."

Benny nodded. "What's the story?" he said.

The northman looked up at him. "The bomb was put together in the house we want."

Benny felt his body tensing up. "Where—local?" he said.

The northman rubbed his eyes. "He's been stashing stuff out there for the past two years. They have everything they want on him now."

He paused. "You know him," he said.

Benny looked at him. His palms sweated. "Who?" he asked.

"Hamilton. The shopkeeper."

"Alec Hamilton? Jesus Christ."

"That's him."

Benny shook his head incredulously. "No. They've got it wrong. It can't be him."

"It's him all right. He has a fucking arsenal out there. Where he has it we don't know. But that's what we're going to find out. That's where the weapons were stashed for the McCarney job, that's where the bomb that killed your mate was assembled. He didn't plant it but next thing to it. He's a bad bastard. Black as your boot Benny."

Hamilton. Alec Hamilton. Solid, dependable Alec Hamilton.

"It's a mistake," Benny began. He broke off as the northman shook his head.

He smiled and flicked away his cigarette. "These people don't make mistakes Benny. He's been checked and double-checked. That's why we've waited."

He paused and said. "The profits from his shop go to the Orange Order."

"How did they find that out?"

"I told you—he goes back a long way. He lived in places besides Carn you know. You wouldn't catch him in this place unless there was money to be made. It's not the first time."

They lapsed into silence and then the northman said, "It has to be Friday. Cooney's throwing his party on Friday so there won't be a stir out in the fields. There's four other men in on this. Northmen. Belfast." Benny nodded.

"Right then. Youse know the terrority better than us. You'll be able to keep your eyes open and give us more time. They'll be staying in a house five miles from the town. I'll let you know everything tomorrow."

The northman turned to go. "Anything you need to know you'll know by tomorrow night. Come Saturday, we'll have put an end to their little game once and for all." He lifted the last crate onto the lorry and went inside.

Benny stared down at the sleeping town. In the distance, beyond the railway, he could see the rolling outline of the Hairy Mountains. Despite himself, his body was cold with anxiety.

These people don't make mistakes.

He hadn't expected it to be someone like Hamilton. It had thrown him off-centre.

But it *was* Hamilton.

And he was in on it now.

XVII

*If you don't love it, leave it, let the song that ahm
a-singin' be a warnin'
When you're runnin' down mah kahmtaree you're a
walkin' on thu' fightin' side o' me . . . .*

The Oklahoma Mountain Boys were in full swing and the music wafted out through the open upstairs windows of the Turnpike Inn. The lead singer wore a JR stetson and dark glasses, winking to the patrons as they filed in. The drummer chewed gum laconically, twirling his sticks in the air. The cymbals crashed as the song finished and the lead singer replaced the microphone.

"Thank y'all ladies and gentlemen, I'd like to welcome you all here to the Turnpike Inn. I sure do hope you're all gonna have a mighty fine time. Me and the boys here are gonna whip up some mighty tunes for y'all so don't forget that the bar's free so don't waste no time get up there and git swillin'. We'd like to continue now with a li'l number called *My Son calls another man Daddy*."

The singer closed his eyes and his face contorted. A group of mature women turned away from the bar counter and lost themselves in the lyric of the song. They shook their heads sadly. Drinks sailed over the counter. The bikers gathered about the huge video screen which blasted out heavy metal rock music over the sound of the band. They mimed with invisible guitars. In a very short time the Turnpike Inn was packed to the door.

There was barely room to breathe. The mature women cheered as the band finished their number. The caretaker of the factory took the stage with his accordeon and four Scots terriers which followed him everywhere. He tripped over a microphone cable and fell on top of his instrument. The dogs climbed on top of him, licking his face. The accordeon squeezed out a screeching discord. The whole pub cheered as he fell again in his efforts to right himself. The dogs barked about his legs. The singer clapped and urged all to join in the applause. "Fuck youse," said the caretaker and began to search for the keys. He started up a rousing march medley in a variety of keys. At a table beside the stage, a young blonde girl sat on the knee of a forty-year-old man, tickling his ear. An assembly line worker stumbled against her and spilt drink over her white dress. She burst out laughing. He looked down at her, his eyes bloodshot and cooed into her face, "Let Me call you Sweetheart . . ." She spluttered into her hands. "She's my cousin," said the forty-year-old man. "She's from England."

"I worked in England," said the assembly line worker. "Do you know Hackney?"

They couldn't hear him over the din of the accordeon and the barking dogs.

"Sit down there," said the forty-year-old man, winking as he handed the blonde girl a cigarette.

"I'm on holidays. I'm from England," she said.

"Hackney. Do you know Hackney?" he cried at the top of his voice.

"I'm from Nottingham. My dad's Irish."

"So you're his cousin. I say, have you any more cousins like that?"

She laughed and threw her head back. Her skirt rode up over her thigh. He squeezed it firmly.

"Oh no. She's the best cousin I have."

Up on the stage the accordeon player was lying on his back and the dogs were lapping up the pools of spilt drink around him. The members of the band lifted him up and eased him off. The dogs bit at their legs angrily. "And now we'd like to ask Mrs Donoghue to give us a verse of a song," announced the singer.

The mature women at the bar clapped and cheered as one of their number blushed and was ushered reluctantly down the length of the bar. The racket died down and she began. *As I was slowly passing, an orphange one day, I stopped just for a minute, to see the children play* . . .

The women went quiet. The men momentarily followed suit but then went back to their arguments with renewed vigour. The television was turned up full for the results of a football match. The heavy metal guitars screeched. The assembly line worker said to the blonde girl, "You'll have a double vodka.

You will. Aren't you on holidays?" She fell back into his waiting arms.

"This is the best night we ever had in Carn. I'm having four brandies next round."

"Get them off you," shouted the bikers at the singer.

She wiggled her ample hips.

Sadie had just got the kids to bed and was settling down in the armchair to watch television when Una arrived.

She had her kid sister with her.

"Well Sadie," she said, "just thought we'd surprise you."

Sadie made a cup of tea as Una explained that her husband had gone to Dublin to visit his brother in hospital. "Make you sick. We were going to the party in the Turnpike tonight. Wouldn't happen any other time. Are you going?"

Sadie hadn't heard anything about it. "No," she said. "Benny never mentioned anything about a party. He's working late at the factory tonight. He's on the nightshift."

"Nightshift? What about the do?"

Sadie shrugged her shoulders. "Benny wouldn't be keen on that. Not after Joe and everything."

They sat in silence watching the television. Then Una said to her sister, "Go on up and see how the kids are, will you?" The young girl left. Una reached in her handbag and took out a noggin of brandy. "I brought you a present Sadie. Get a couple of glasses there."

She filled the glasses to the brim. "Cheers," she said.

"Cheers," said Sadie, taken aback by this unexpected display of exuberance.

"When I was coming down the place was wild. You could hear the music from our house. They've a free bar you know." She thought about it for a moment and then said, "Sadie—would you like to go up to it?"

Sadie replied, "How can I? Tara was like a weasel all day."

"Can't you let her babysit? She was due to mind ours but my mother's with them so she's free. Come on Sadie—once in your life."

Sadie drank. "Are you sure? She wouldn't mind?"

"Of course not. Just slip her a few quid. Come on Sadie—Jesus when do we ever get the chance to go out. Stuck in from morning to night. We'd be stupid to let it pass us by."

Sadie held back and almost declined. She looked at Una's eager face.

"Why should we let it pass us by?"

She looked down at her slippered feet. At the kitchen in disarray. The flickering screen. "Okay. Just wait till I get changed," she said.

She dabbed perfume behind her ears. The brandy went through her, filled her with anticipation. Before she went downstairs, she checked the children again.

"You're sure you'll be all right?" she said to Una's sister.

"Of course she will," said Una, "doesn't she mind ours? Come on. That's a fantastic dress Sadie. Jesus you look smashing."

They closed the door behind them and set off for the Turnpike Inn.

❧

The tepid air of the bar hit them in the face as soon as they opened the door. The drinkers were six-deep at the bar struggling to be heard over the noise. "Last orders now, you pay from now on," cried the barman. "A treble whiskey and five pints of lager," cried a voice in the wilderness. The band were well down one of the spot prizes which they had clandestinely awarded to themselves and were playing in a variety of different keys. The lead singer burst into laughter at incongruous moments and the others discarded their instruments helplessly. The lyrics of songs were interchanged at random. The accordeon player's dogs wandered around in search of their slumbering master and stray pools of spilt alcohol. *Gonna get mah motorsickle and head out out on the road,* screamed the vast image of the heavy metal rocker on the video. The bikers passed a joint from hand to hand and horse-played on the tables. They climbed on each other's backs. The blonde English girl was crying and laughing at the same time as she crawled under the table searching for her contact lenses. The two men were clinging to each other like lovers, pledging lifelong friendship. "You're one of the best, one of the best." "And so are you, so are you."

The English girl stood forlornly in the middle of the floor. "I can't find them," she sobbed. "And look at my dress. My dress is ruined." Her white dress was stained with Guinness and cigarette ash.

"Come over here cousin and get this down you. You won't know yourself then." He held up a replenished glass of spirits and threw back his head, rocking with laughter. His companion shook his head and wept. "You're one of the funniest men in this town. Come on over here cousin."

The English girl sat on his knee with her wet hair falling down on her face. She chewed her nail and dabbed her eyes with a tissue. Beneath the television a group of football supporters waved scarves and held pint glasses aloft. On the television screen above them, the prime minister adjusted his spectacles and, reading from a script, morosely confirmed that every man woman and child in the Republic of Ireland owed ten thousand pounds each.

The caretaker sat between two of the mature women. His limbs flopped about him heavily and he tried to focus his eyes. One of the women felt inside his open shirt. "It must be hard for you. Cooney is too bloody cute."

"Hard is right," sniggered her companion. "Hard in all the right places."

The other woman laid a hand on his shoulder and whispered into his ear, "Buy me a little half-one. Will you?"

"This place is mad," said Una Lacey. "I never seen it like this."

"Two double brandies," called the barman.

Una paid for the drinks and they sat down. Sadie was taken aback by the cacophony of the bar so she drank quickly to steady her nerves. The mature woman was now on the stage bumping and grinding to the sound of hissing cymbals.

She raised her dress above her knee slowly and dropped it again. The whole bar squealed with delight. The drummer pounded. Sweat rolled down his cheeks. "The minute you walked in the joint . . ." sang the woman. The guitarist made lewd gestures with his right arm. She rotated her backside. Hats flew in the air. Her dress fell off her shoulder. The footballers cried, *Irriwaddy Irriwaddy Yip Yip Yip!* It fell in a crumpled heap on the floor. At the counter her husband fumed with rage and shame.

"Jesus Mary and Joseph, she must be out of her brain," said Una. Sadie ordered two more brandies. "You're getting through these Sadie. Fair play to you. We should go out more often."

"What would Blast Morgan have to say about this?" she laughed, the warmth of the brandy coursing through her.

More more more more more more more more

The crowd was in hysterics. Fired by their enthusiasm, the woman called for a friend to join her. They bumped and grinded together, shaking their breasts at the men under the stage.

The bikers took over the bar and began to serve

drinks free. "Everything on Jame Cooney. Right—who's first?"

A pint glass came out of nowhere and splintered against Davy Crockett's coonskin cap.

"Fuck Cooney!" cried someone. "Don't mention Cooney—that's what I think of James Cooney!"

The drummer's knuckles bled. The dogs licked the paralytic body of their accordeon-playing master under a table. Some of the normally less extrovert workers had now joined the bikers, who looked on mirthfully as they struggled without success to inhale the marijuana. The primary school teacher leaned over to a former pupil explaining the complexities of the political situation to him. He listened respectfully but didn't hear a word the schoolmaster said.

An argument started up among the footballers. What had caused it? Why had Carn Rovers not had a victory in fifteen successive matches? The rapid decline in the club's fortunes had continued unabated in the past year and thrown the ranks into utter confusion. And now, as had become common in the bars and other public places, friends who had once been unquestioningly loyal to the club, argued bitterly among themselves. But even those who had been with the club from the early days could not ignore what was now in most people's minds—it was the mismanagement and bad decision-making of Pat Lacey that had been responsible for many of the defeats and the continuing low morale. He had lost his touch, they whispered and ought to be fired. It was sad but it was true. They sought for evidence of loyalty to him in order to lay the brunt of their recriminations on the backs of his supporters. But there were none to be found and they only succeeded in covering the same old sour ground again. In the end, like battle-weary soldiers, they linked arms reluctantly and began to sing, *Carn Rovers Carn Rovers we're the best team in the land* . . .

A pint of beer dripped down John F. Kennedy's smiling face. The video screen went blank and when the picture returned a crazed youth in an asbestos suit was setting a series of young women alight. He met them in singles bars, lured them to his home and burnt them alive. They turned from the woman on the stage and gave their attention to this for a while. They stared open-mouthed as he applied his flame thrower to the feet of a trussed-up girl.

"What do you think of that master?" cried one of the footballers to the teacher.

"Shut up or he'll send you to the priest."

"To Father Tom? He's too busy giving it to his housekeeper!"

"Tell us about Patrick Pearse and De Valera master, like you used to. What are they up to these days?"

"Waving their dicks for Ireland master!"

They cheered as the schoolmaster, at a loss for words, put on his coat and fumbled his way past them out into the street.

Feedback from the speakers whistled as the mature woman made her way back to her seat. The band struck up again, and exhorted all to join in this time. The crowd clapped along, belting out the chorus with gusto.

We're on the one road sharing the one load
We're on the road to God know's where
We're on the one road sharing the one load
But we're together now who cares?
Northmen southmen comrades all
Dublin Belfast Cork and Donegal
We're on the one road singing along
Singing a soldier's song.

The footballers chanted, *Here We Go Here We Go . . .*

"Got my motorsickle outside and I'm heading out on the road!" sang the bikers.

The songs collided with each other and made no sense. But no one was about to give an inch and with each new verse they hurled themselves further into the chaos.

Una and Sadie were far gone. They put their arms around one another and said that they were best friends, always had been. We go back years, they said to one another. Una leaned over to a teenage girl sitting beside them and said, "When we were your age, we were wild. The things we used to get up to. We didn't give a damn. Did we Sadie?"

"Una was the first girl in Carn to wear a mini . . ."

The teenage girl looked blankly at them.

Una went to the bar and ordered two more drinks. When she came back she found Sadie deep in conversation with a man whose face she recognised. "Una—do you remember Don? He used to work in Poultry Products? Don—you remember Una."

"Hi."

She sat with the drinks.

"I couldn't believe it when I saw you sitting there. Sadie Rooney—it seems so long ago now . . ." said Don.

"I barely recognised you Don. The tan," Sadie said.

"Yeah. I'm gone a long time. I never expected to see you here. It's not always like this, is it? Or maybe I've been away too long . . ." He gestured with his head at the disarray behind him.

"Where are you now Don?" asked Una, moulding her words carefully to offset the effect of the alcohol.

"Aussie. We're in Sydney. This is my first trip home. I brought a mate with me. Here he comes. I've been telling him all about the place. But he never expected this."

The Australian sat down and placed the drinks on the table.

"Here are two friends of mine from the old days. Two Elvis fans."

"Hi. I'm Paul."

"Well Sadie—how have you been? You know Paul—this girl—could she sing Elvis—we used to go out to the Hairy Mountains, a gang of us—we were only kids. Jesus—she could do an Elvis impersonation—eh Sadie?"

Sadie reddened. "Oh I don't know about that . . ."

"So what's been happening around Carn then—apart from these lunatics . . ."

Una started the ball rolling and Sadie got into the swing of things. The Australian insisted on buying all the drink. The table filled up with glasses. "Any fan of The King is okay by me," he said.

"Bebopalula she's my baby," sang Sadie.

"Never mind us, we're well on," said Una.

"I'll tell you something Una," said Don, "you'd really enjoy the life out there. Sydney—it's the place to be. And it's easy to get in there now . . . did you ever think about it?"

"I was thinking of going to London," said Sadie, then collapsed into nonsensical laughter.

"We'd look well in Sydney all right," said Una.

"There you go," said the Australian, setting more drinks down on the table. Sadie felt as if she was about to faint. The noise and the smoke swirled.

One of the bikers stood up on the counter and with a wild look in his eyes cried, "Let's show Mr Cooney what we think of him and his factory!" He lifted the microwave oven above his shoulders and sent it crashing against the drinks display against the wall. "There's your present from Carn, Mr Fly Boy Cooney!"

Another biker slashed the face of John F. Kennedy with a snooker cue. On the video screen the rows of women on meat hooks in the maniac's house went up in flames as he removed his asbestos mask and twitched excitedly.

The footballers continued, *Here we go-oh! Here we Go!*

"Cooney betrayed Carn!" cried a boning-hall worker at the microphone. Behind the bar the mirror was smashed to smithereens.

"She's my cousin," said Marty to a neighbour, explaining the prone figure of the unconcunscious girl on the floor. "I think she might have had one over the eight." He broke into laughter and squeezed the mystified neighbour's arm. "What do you think?" he said to the assembly worker who was askew across the table, "One too many maybe?"

The dogs barked, forgotten by their master who was still dead to the world.

"You bitch. You dirty bitch," said the mature woman's husband bitterly.

Then the policeman appeared in the doorway, followed by three of his colleagues. A hush fell. The bikers squashed the joint underfoot. The musicians began to drag their cables across the stage and pack up their instruments. The policemen moved to the centre of the floor. Slowly people drifted as anonymously as they could to the exit. The policemen stared at the wreckage that confronted them. They turned their attention to the bikers. The football chant stopped abruptly.

"Reckon it's time to get moving," said Don, finishing up his drink.

"Come on Sadie," Una nudged Sadie who looked up emptily. "The police."

They made their way out the back. Outside the Pizza Parlour the chant had begun again. The bikers kicked a dustbin down the main street. *We're on the one road sharing the one load we're on the road to God knows where* . . . they sang, muted now.

They stood in the snow.

"Seems a shame to go home now. After all that. Just getting to know you again . . ." said Don.

"Where could we go?" shrugged Una. "You know this place . . ."

"What about the Hairy Mountains—just for old

time's sake. We're going back to Aussie tomorrow ..."

Una hesitated. "What do you say Sadie?"

Somewhere at the back of her mind, everything she cared about tugged at Sadie.

"Just for old times sake Sadie ..." said Don.

The Australian felt in his coat pocket and produced a small tin. He opened it to reveal a nugget of cannabis.

"Just for old time's sake Sadie. We never had a chance to get to know each other right."

"Okay," said Sadie.

"The car's over here," said the Australian.

"Why not?" whispered Una in Sadie's ear as they crossed the road. "We'll be dead long enough."

They climbed into the back seat and the rock and roll music from the stereo pulsated as they turned out of the main street and sped off towards the railway and the Hairy Mountains.

XVIII

It was after one when Benny arrived at the house. The northmen were inside playing cards. "Benny," said one of them in a sharp Belfast accent. He joined them at the table. "Okay then," the Belfast man began, "this is what we do."

The northmen were to search the house. They would find the arms dump if it was there. If it wasn't, they would take the outhouses one by one. The northman from the factory and Benny were to keep their eyes open outside, one at the back, one at the front. The whole thing was to take no more than half an hour. Benny was handed a sawn-off shotgun. "You'll need this too." He threw him a woollen balaclava mask.

"Right—time we were moving."

They donned their masks and checked their weapons. For the first ime, the enormity of what they were doing hit Benny and he felt nauseous. His hands were clammy and his head throbbed. He tried to get rid of Sadie and think of Joe.

"Okay then Benny?"

"Right."

The car drove slowly down the lane on to the main road.

Alec Hamilton's wife screamed when the door of the house was kicked open and a masked man caught her husband by the throat and pinned him against the wall. Her whole body began to shake when another man pressed the barrel of a pistol against her temple. Her daughter was hauled downstairs from her bedroom and flung on the couch.

"You know why we're here. Talk!"

The elderly woman began to cry.

"For the love of God . . ." pleaded Alec Hamilton.

"Where is it?"

"What are you talking about? Please—my wife . . ." The pistol butt bruised his cheek. "You have the wrong house. There's nothing here. Please—you must have the wrong place."

"This is the place all right, Hamilton. Where have you it? Where have you the ironmongery for your Brit friends?"

"Please."

"Tell us now when you have the chance or we'll take the place apart brick by fucking brick . . . where is the dump Hamilton?"

"You're wrong. There's nothing here." He was flung to the ground.

"Take up the floorboards. Take the place apart. You're a dead man if we find it Hamilton."

Ornaments were swept from the mantelpiece. Drawers were thrown to the floor. A picture of the queen was dropped into the fire.

"Where the fuck have you it Hamilton? If we don't find it soon, your wife there can start praying for you . . ."

XIX

"It was nice of you to come Pat," said Josie and smiled. Pat Lacey was uneasy, passing his hat from hand to hand as he stood in the centre of the kitchen. Josie was unsteady on her feet and her dressing gown was half open. She drank from the brandy glass and said, "I wasn't sure if you'd be able to make it. I'm sure you have a lot of visitors at this time of the year."

"Her people . . . always call. It's all near over now anyway." He lit a cigarette with trembling hands.

"Yes. It's nice to have the family around you at Christmas Pat." She poured him a full glass of brandy.

He scratched his neck with his index finger and said, "There's . . . nothing wrong Josie, is there?"

She handed him the drink, puckered up her nose and looked at him with misty eyes. "Wrong? No, of course not. What makes you think there's something wrong?"

"The note you sent me—you never did that before, like."

"I missed you Pat." She moved closer to him. She

touched his cheek. He looked away. "We're missing the big party in the Turnpike Inn Pat. Don't you want to go to Mr Cooney's party?"

"I was thinking, maybe I could be getting along there now—I don't want to leave it too late like. I'd be as well to get home early after it, in case they'd think there's something wrong at home."

"Oh you're not going yet Pat. There's no need to rush. I got a bottle of this especially for you."

"I said I'd be there about nine."

"Ssh." She put her tongue into his mouth and felt him shiver. She eased away from him and held the brandy glass to his lips. The liquid slowly went down. She filled it up again.

"Ah I think I have enough Josie," he said.

She put her arm around his neck. She tickled his nose with her nail and laughed, stumbling backwards. She laughed aloud. Pat Lacey had never seen her like this before. His eyes darted anxiously to the window.

"Oh Pat, a big man like you. I thought all you men could hold your drink. I thought a big tough man like Pat Lacey could put down more than one wee glass of brandy, now. Come on Pat, don't let me down." She ruffled his hair. "It's only a little bitty drink Pat."

He reddened as she looked deep into his eyes. She kept her eyes there and would not look away. The brandy went through him as she held the glass to his lips. She stroked his cheek. Her dressing-gown fell open. Slowly Pat Lacey went to his knees and she pressed his head to her abdomen. She cooed to him in the voice she kept for him. "You were glad to get my note, weren't you Pat? You think you weren't but you were. Were you afraid she'd find out? Who were you afraid of Pat?"

His breathing was rapid beneath her.

"Was it Jack Murphy? Were you afraid maybe Jack Murphy would find out? There's no need to be afraid of Jack. You could trust Jack. You could tell him anything Pat. I say you could tell him anything."

She tightened her grip on the back of his neck. He whimpered.

"Jack's a man like yourself. He'd understand. Men understand one another." She lifted him up gently and began to unbutton his shirt.

"How's Mrs Lacey these days Pat? Making you nice dinners?" She plucked at the grey hairs on his chest. "You don't bother with the dinners when you come out to Josie's, mm?"

The Sacred Heart lamp flickered in the silence. Pat Lacey could not bring himself to look her in the eye.

"You'll have another drink with me Pat, won't you? That's better than any dinner. I'm lonely for someone to drink with. That's why I dropped you the little note. I knew you wouldn't let me down."

She took the bottle from the table and spilt some of it down his chest. She smiled and slowly began to rub it into his skin. She rubbed it into his face and his eyes. "Does she do that for you Pat? Does she give you a drink? Does she?" She cried out, *Does she?*

He began to weep. "Please Josie—I don't know what's going on . . . what are you doing Josie? You're not yourself . . . you don't look well Josie . . ." The bottle fell on the armchair. Josie was unsteady on her feet. She settled herself against the heater. She stared at him without speaking.

He looked back at her helplessly. He pleaded with her to speak to him. Then his words became heavy and slurred. His eyelids drooped and his head fell. Josie had dosed the brandy with her librium and the tryptasol the doctor had given her. Words trailed out of his mouth but had no meaning. He reached out to her but she backed away. He clutched at the arm of the chair. He managed to say *please* before he fell to the floor.

Josie trembled. She was cold all over. She took another bottle from the cupboard and sat down to try and hold her mind together. It took her over a minute to pour the glass.

When Pat Lacey awoke, a fog swirled in the room. The tiny flickering flame and the pitying eyes were gone. He tried to focus. Above him huge spidery cracks intersected on the bedroom ceiling. He saw the shape of Josie Keenan standing in the corner. He could hear her breathing. But she didn't move. She was just standing there, in the shadows, looking down at him.

He made to get up and found that he couldn't budge. His hands were tied to the bedstead. She had tied his hands. Fear shot through him. She stood there looking.

"Josie. What did you do? Josie—what are you doing to me? Please Josie—I'm not well . . . whatever you put in it—I have a bad heart . . ." He cried out with frustration when she did not answer him. He cried out over and over. He pulled at the bonds. Then she approached him and what he saw sickened and terrified him. She was wearing a tattered old rag of a dress, sizes too small for her. Her hair was matted and uncombed. She muttered and mumbled to herself as if he weren't in the room. He got very afraid. "Josie— I had nothing to do with it. Murphy told me—it was the barman. Murphy's destroyed over it. That's the truth Josie . . . I'll go to the police myself about it . . . Murphy was going to tell them everything."

She sat down on the bed beside him and looked at him. Her eyes were like empty caves. She stroked his cheek again. "Ssh wee pet," she said.

She held a bottle of pills in her hand. She emptied them on to the bed. "I have nice little sweets here Pat. Sweets for Josie." She swallowed a handful of them. She retched. Then she smiled at him. "You don't like me in this dress Pat, I can see. Phil liked it. Phil Brady was very fond of it. It's a pity you don't like it after me putting it on specially for you . . .' course then you're not like them . . . you're different . . . you're not so fond of the young girls."

Her cheeks were moist and raw. She cried and laughed at the same time. She fell onto his stomach and cried, "Poor Pat, poor old Pat." Then she stumbled to the table and called over to him. "It was you sent him Pat. You told him all about the games. But you changed things around a little bit, didn't you?"

"Please Josie—for the love of Jesus. Take these off me. Cut this rope . . ."

She came over to the bed. His whole body went rigid as he saw the bread-knife in her hand. She touched his cheek with it. "You want me to cut them? Cut them with this?"

"Josie—I never did anything to you. I never sent anyone near you. I'd never harm you. I get afraid sometimes but as God is my judge I would never harm a hair on your head, that's the truth . . ."

"You and the Buyer Keenan, you should get talking. He liked the things you like. He showed me everything."

Her voice began to splinter like glass and she put her hands to her face. Pat Lacey only heard part of what she said as she sat there with her face covered, the knife lying between them. She cried fitfully. "There's no skin on God's sweet earth like the skin of a woman and God help me I've nobody now our Cassie is gone . . . Cassie please help me Cassie please help me . . ."

She stood up and tried to cross the room but she fell back against the heater. She crawled across the floor. She came back to the bed on all fours. She pulled at the bedcovers but they came loose and she fell to the floor again.

"Cassie please—take me out of this world . . . please take me wherever you are for the love of Christ . . . Cassie wherever you are."

She vomited. Sweat poured out of Pat Lacey as he worked on the cord. It bit into his wrist as he strained with his ebbing strength. She blubbered at the end of the bed, she saw nothing. His hand came free. He grabbed the bread-knife and cut his other arm free. Suddenly Josie looked up, her hair smeared with sick and her lip quivering. "Please Pat," she said helplessly, "please," reaching out to him.

He got his clothes and fumbled frantically for the door latch.

A light burned at the far side of the valley.

He began to run, his head spinning.

It was all over now. He would have to phone an ambulance. He couldn't leave her there, her head was gone, there was no knowing what she would do to herself.

He had ruined himself.

Everything would come out now.

XX

The Australian inhaled the joint and passed it to Una. She giggled as she smoked, tears in her eyes. Don drummed on the dashboard in time to the music.

"Remember those summers we used to come out here? Lie here all day . . . remember Sadie?"

Sadie nodded and took the joint from Una. The car was filled with smoke.

"Pity we didn't have this stuff then," said Una.

The Australian put his arm around her. "Why don't you come and see Bondi Beach with me Una?" he said.

"I'd be gone in a shot," said Una. "What about you Sadie?"

Sadie was too drowsy to reply.

"We'd be a right looking pair on Bondi Beach now, all the way from Abbeyville Gardens."

"Greatest country in the world," said Don, nodding affirmatively to himself. "Greatest country in the world."

XXI

Pat Lacey crossed the field.

The light was burning in Alec Hamilton's house. How would he explain it to Hamilton? How could he explain what he was doing there at that time of night?

Jesus.

He thought of leaving her there. How could he be connected? They wouldn't believe her.

He couldn't. Not in that state. God knows what could happen to her.

Jesus Jesus.

The house rose up across the field. He couldn't run much further.

In the farmyard Benny waited. A tarpaulin flapped in the light wind. His hands were wet. Inside he heard crockery crash against a wall. The voices became increasingly louder. He shifted from foot to foot.

Why couldn't they just find it and get the hell out, what were they doing? What was taking them so long?

Then the dread that had been stalking him began to take root as he thought, *It's the wrong place, there's nothing here* . . .

He started as a sheet of tin rattled against an outhouse wall. He tried to settle himself. His body had a skin of cold sweat. His stomach turned over.

You lying bitch! cried a voice inside.

Then a woman crying.

Benny suddenly became aware of how tightly his teeth were clenched together.

Come on for Christ's sake and let's get out of here . . .

In the distance a dog barked. Then at the side of the outhouse there was a rustling sound.

He stiffened.

He heard it again.

Was it the northman? What was he doing there? It was an animal. A dog or a sheep at the bushes. He strained to see but there was only darkness. Inside the woman cried out again and the Belfast voice spat, *If you don't tell me I'll do it right here and now you bitch*.

Benny said to himself, *Easy easy* and waited for it to go but then close by he heard it again, and despite himself he cried out, *Who is it who's there?*

He only caught a glimpse of the face before the bushes sprang back and the man turned and ran. Benny shouted after him, *Stay where you are stay where you are.*

The man struggled to climb the wire fence back into the field. He wavered.

Benny called again. He was in the field and starting

to run. Benny jerked backwards and the sound became bone breaking in his head. The man fell. There was silence for a split second then the voices inside cried out, *What was that what the fuck was that? There's someone shooting at us get down!*

Benny stood back. The tarpaulin flapped and the sheet of tin rattled. Inside the house the lights were doused. There was no sound from the field where the man was. The northman came to the front of the house. The shotgun hung limp in Benny's arm. His legs were about to buckle under him. The door opened.

"What was that? Who fired that shot? Where did it come from?" Benny gestured towards the field. They climbed the wire. It looked like a pile of old clothes lying in the ditch. The northman paled. He tilted Pat Lacey's face upwards. It was covered in blood. "Jesus!" he said. "Jesus Christ!"

His voice quivered as he stood up. He turned to Benny and spat, "You bastard—you stupid bastard! Now you've gone and done it good and proper!"

He ran back inside. The Hamiltons were on their knees praying. The northmen lost their minds. They furiously erased all the fingerprints. They took the Hamiltons outside. They soaked the furniture in petrol. Benny, half-dazed, wiped fingerprints from the window. The northman pushed him out of the way and snapped bitterly, "You've done your fucking bit pal. Stay out of it . . ."

The Hamiltons stood in their nightclothes and watched the house go up in flames. A tarry smell began to fill the valley.

The northman pointed his pistol as them. "Walk. Get walking. And don't stop. You're a lucky man tonight Hamilton. We know you have it somewhere—we'll get you . . ."

The northman pulled off his mask and shouted. "It's every man for himself now. Move! Separate for fuck's sake!"

In a split second the farmyard had emptied and Benny Dolan flinging the shotgun from him, sickened, and unable to hold his thoughts together, stumbled forward into the darkness.

XXII

Josie clutched at the table to steady herself. She feared she was going to vomit again. A searing pain went through her head. The open door swung idly.

Across the valley the sky burned.

You better say your prayers now. Say your prayers to the Sacred Heart . . . Look there He is, looking down on you, a right-looking sketch you are with sick on your face, your hands shaking and your mind not your own. You made your bed and now you can lie in it.

"Pat—help me! Please Pat where are you?"

The door swung. The smoke rose up into the sky above the Hairy Mountains. *What was it? What did it mean?*

She stumbled as she went out across the field, calling his name over and over, answered only by her own voice.

XXIII

The shot rang out and rolled across the Hairy Mountains.

Don switched the radio off sharply. "What the hell was that?"

He opened the car door. He went across the field. Then he turned and beckoned to the Australian. "Come on—let's see what's going on."

They got out of the car. Thick smoke was drifting above the valley.

"We better get the fuck out of here," said Don, whitefaced.

Sadie went cold when she looked down into the valley. The Hamilton house was in flames. Two men in balaclava masks ran towards the woods. The smell of the fire was beginning to drift over the fields.

"Jesus," said the Australian, as Don went back hastily to the car. He started the engine and called through the open window. "Come on."

Una pulled Sadie's arm and said, "Let's get out quick Sadie . . ."

Sadie had turned to follow them when she saw

Josie emerge from the woods and cross the fields in the direction of the house. She cried out with all her strength. "Josie—Josie!"

They called to her again from the car. Down in the valley, Josie stumbled and rose again, still making for the house.

Far away Sadie heard the engine and the sound of their voices as she ran down into the valley.

❧

The voice that called wasn't Cassie's voice. With all the strength that was left in her, Josie called her name and wept bitterly when they came at her again.

Call all you like she won't come. Why should she come when she never did before, no matter what lies you tell yourself. Where was she when you came home from your school? Where was she then Keenan? The door open to the fields and the dishes stinking. She did as she pleased and cared for nothing or no one. Saint Cassie was a lazy bitch and the whole town knew it. She came from a bad crowd, couldn't be good. That's you and all belonging to you. Look at you, the cut of you like an auld mangy dog lying in a ditch. How will your precious Cassie explain that to her good friend the Sacred Heart of Jesus, what will she tell Him about her precious daughter lying there half-daft and the track of every tramp in the country left on her? She'll tell Him you're not hers, that's what she'll tell Him. For you never were Keenan, there never was a day with catkins. There never was a check dress or forget-me-nots.

For-get-me-nots my eye, you dreamed it all, you wanted it to be that way didn't you? What day did you and her ever have? You dreamed it all, every word. The Buyer Keenan beat her all right and beat her he should have for she never made a dinner, out half the day and the house a filthy den, that was your Cassie, left you and him for days while she walked the roads and pleased herself, and what would you expect from a hoor only a hoor. And the Sacred Heart, He'd look well with the likes of her. He'd have nothing to do with a slut like her. The Buyer and her were well met, wasn't one but knew it, catch them saying it but they knew it right enough. You'd no mother Keenan, if you had where is she now?

A beam fell in the burning house.

The voice called, *Josie Josie*. Who was it? It was Cassie calling, *Josie Josie do you hear me wee pet, don't mind their bitter lies they're jealous always were, they hated us, they hated me for I wouldn't taint my tongue with lies the like of theirs that's why they hate you, it's all bitter lies all of it and don't let me tell you different. I did all I could for you and him and now I'm here wee Josie, look over here, that day is here again, you remember, the sun and the catkins and the sky blue and never-ending. There's just you and me now wee Josie just you and Cassie Keenan. I've waited all this time.*

Cassie smiled, it was the saint smile that Josie knew, the smile it had always been, and Josie saw it all now, their words were lies, all bad lies that faded now as Cassie's arms outstretched and Josie fell, a child again, back into the warmth of her mother's body.

The smoke choked her and Cassie's arms folded about her.

Sadie did not reach her in time. She stood there before the flames trying to scream, her face raw. Then she fainted.

When she awoke she found herself lying on a makeshift bed covered with a coat. Above her a female officer proffered a mug of coffee. Somewhere a typewriter clacked.

"Where am I—I have to see my kids. Where are my kids?"

A redfaced man in a raincoat grinned. "You'll see your kids when we're ready," he said. "You have a lot of talking to do before you see anyone, you Provo bitch."

He turned and went out, closing the door loudly behind him. The policewoman smiled.

Sadie took the mug with trembling hands.

XXIV

The news of the shooting of Pat Lacey spread like wildfire. No two versions of the story were the same. The charred shell of the Hamilton house was surrounded by police and military. The workers in the factory listened hungrily as a neighbour of the Hamiltons repeatedly described the sound of the shot, the cries, and the crackling of the flames. The northmen had managed to escape. Benny Dolan had been found wandering blind on the border.

Pat Lacey shot dead.

No one could believe it.

His daughter Una had been taken to hospital suffering from shock. The town was struck dumb. Nobody wanted to raise their voice in case they might somehow be implicated. In the factory the name of Benny Dolan was on everyone's mind and on nobody's lips. Maisie Lynch broke the silence by announcing that she had always known there was something about Benny Dolan. "Let's face it," she said. "His father was a murderer." The famous politician returned to the town and spoke bitterly on the television, saying that it was time to take off the kid gloves and root out the vermin, anyone that would hunt an old man and his aged wife out of their house in the dead of night was nothing more than scum. Was this what we had sunk to? he asked, and the people of Carn felt that he was speaking directly to them from the television screen.

Under cover of darkness the Dolan plaque was broken in two. It lay forlorn in the square, the name Dolan smeared with tar. Over a period of two days there was a constant stream of visitors to the Lacey home where everything Benny Dolan had ever said or done was re-evaluated at length. Una Lacey, heavily sedated, stared dead-eyed at the relatives and friends of her father who lowered their eyes and weakly shook her hand. Over cups of tea, football matches long since past were relived, the night the cup had come home to Carn and not a man woman or child had slept a wink, Pat Lacey carried on a victory parade through the streets with the silver trophy held aloft. Coach trips to away matches came alive in the kitchen, then faded away again to a distant time, as if they belonged solely now with the body of Pat Lacey. The members of the Anti-Divorce League had a special wreath made and delivered to the house. The body was taken from the mortuary and brought to the church where Pat Lacey lay beneath the stained glass Sacred Heart with his arms crossed in the padded box, his pinched face fixed with a faint smile, beside him, in an unopened coffin, the body of Josie Keenan.

The double funeral wound its way through the streets. The Pride of Carn Marching Band played behind the hearse as the cortege wound its way towards the cemetery on the hill above the town.

James Cooney, Father Kelly and the National Secretary of the Anti-Divorce League walked silently behind the band. The curtains were discreetly drawn in all the houses. The shops and business premises were shuttered and barred.

The requiem twisted its way through the tiny streets and alleyways of the town, fanning out across the snowcapped fields of the hinterland. The town became an empty shell as they drifted in silence towards the cemetery. The Secretary of the Anti-Divorce League stood by the open grave and struggled with the wind and a flapping piece of notepaper. His words opened out solemnly above the supplicant, despondent heads of the mourners. The country, he said, was under attack from forces that were all the more formidable because they were in many cases, unseen. Great changes had taken place in Carn and in many other small towns throughout the country, almost without us realising it. Once upon a time, in communities such as this one, there was such a thing as the common good. The personal interests of the individual were secondary in the past to what was perceived to be the good of the community as a whole. But now, all that has changed. People are only interested in what society has to offer them. They are not concerned with what they might be able to do for their neighbour, what they might be able to offer the community. We have become a selfish, irresponsible, materialistic society. We are no longer a caring people. The decay has already set in in many areas of life in this country. Already we are seeing the signs of internal collapse that have so visibly affected other countries—broken homes, crime, greed. But there are people in this country, he went on, who had pledged themselves to the continuation of the values our society once held dear. People who believe that these values are worth fighting for, no matter how unfashionable it may seem. Pat Lacey, my dear friends, was such a man. He was not a man who subscribed to the notion of the ME society. He was a man whose selflessness and dedication knew no bounds. He always had time for everyone. He gave his time unthinkingly to many of the organisations in this town, in particular to the football club, Carn Rovers, which he built up almost single-handedly from nothing. He was a man I myself met on many occasions in connection with our work and I never failed to be deeply impressed by his honesty and sincerity. What a pity his life had to be so tragically cut short by a murderer's bullet. But Pat Lacey would not be the sort of man to bow down before these callous, self-appointed, so-called patriots. He would say to us—let us stand up to them—let us decide what kind of a just society we want—one that does not lust after power and material possessions, that cherishes its children and the family unit above all else—this is the kind of society he wanted . . . and the kind of society, dear friends, that he died for.

The speaker crossed himself and bowed his head. Una Lacey broke down and had to be carried from the graveside. "That bitch's husband killed my father," she screamed helplessly. Sadie stood by the cemetery gate and clutched her daughter's hand tightly to prevent her dropping in a faint. Then the priest began to speak. His voice drifted on the wind down into the streets of the town where Pat Lacey had spent his entire life. A stray dog nosed in the tumbled bins behind the Railway Hotel. The windows of the Turnpike Inn had been blacked out and above the door a sign read CLOSED UNTIL FURTHER NOTICE.

The jeweller's clock stood suspended at three. The broken pump skitted its umbrella of water across the cracked paving slabs. The priest's words seemed to carry for miles. "I remember the first trophy that Carn Rovers brought home. We lit a fire in the square. There were children dancing. Musicians from the town played jigs and reels. The silver band here played for us all in the square. The captain made his speech. It was Pat Lacey's big night. The first time Carn Rovers had brought a trophy home in thirty years. And there were many nights like that afterwards. There were many nights like that afterwards for one reason and one reason only—the hard work and dedication of Patrick Lacey. There are not many men like him. There have not been many in the past and there will not be many in the future. It was because of him, and men like him, that this town became great. It was because of him that Carn became the queen of the county. And perhaps it will, if his memory is to mean anything to us, one day become great once more."

The priest lowered his head and paused for a moment in silence. Then he said, "May he rest in peace."

The rosary began and the deadening chant filled the cemetery. As Josie Keenan's coffin was lowered into the clay, a woman looked up from her prayerbook and whispered, "Do you see that man over there? That's Vincent Culligan. He's a big building contractor in England now."

The tall grey-haired man in the tweed suit stared ahead of him, expressionless and oblivious of her comments. James Cooney stood by the cemetery gate with his BMW parked at a discreet distance where it would neither appear ostentatious nor go unnoticed by the mourners. Beside him the politican shifted from foot to foot and rubbed his gloved hands together. A handful of earth tumbled on both coffins and the Pride of Carn Marching Band began to move back towards the town where a number of the old and infirm who had been unable to make the journey to the cemetery stood white-faced on crutches and geriatric walkers in the shadows of hallways and upstairs windows. The requiem seemed to cling to the town for days after, its echoes hanging vaguely in the air, like a thin fog that would not dissipate.

Maisie Lynch led a torchlit procession through the streets at midnight, reading out her Poem for Peace in the square. It was attended by hundreds of people from the neighbouring counties and widely reported in the national newspapers.

There were bitter scenes at the court where Benny Dolan was sentenced to life imprisonment. Sadie was attacked by a number of women when she appeared in the doorway. Her hair was pulled and her face scratched. She was showered with spittle as a policeman helped her into a patrol car. When the workers saw Benny's photograph in the morning newspaper, they carefully inspected every detail of his face and said to each other, "Look at those eyes. They're the eyes of a killer. I never liked him. There was always something odd about him."

He was never spoken of again while the factory remained open.

In the months that followed, when the people of the town encountered Sadie in the street, waiting with her children for the coach that would take them to the maximum security prison where she would spend an hour with her husband under the cold eye of the warder, they either hurried brusquely past her or made a reluctant, half-heard remark about the weather or the lengthening of the evenings.

In Abbeyville Gardens she rarely received any visitors and any conversations she had through chance, unavoidable meetings with neighbours were confined to stiff, good-mannered exchanges at which their time in the large, anonymous housing estate had made them adept. The construction of a new conservatory or the recent repeat of an American mini-series were consistent safeguards against tense silences that might result from chance meetings with awkward neighbours such as Sadie Dolan. For the people in Abbeyville Gardens, having only come to

Carn in recent years and with their roots in other places, the deaths of Pat Lacey and Josie Keenan affected their lives in the same way as would reports on the evening television news of natural disasters and horrific train crashes in distant, irrelevant countries. When their names were mentioned, only the merest flicker of recognition passed across their faces.

Sadie to them was nothing more or less than anyone else. She did not invade their privacy and they did not invade hers. She was the woman with the two children in number thirty-four.

Sadie gave all her time to her children now and whenever the black moods came down around her, she fought them back bitterly, no matter what it took out of her. She did it for Benny and for them. She wrote weekly to her husband to keep up her strength.

Father Kelly called a number of times and told her to put her trust in God. He told her that He never closed a door but He opened a window. Sadie smiled distantly and stared out the window at the neat rows of saplings and the array of pedal cars and toys scattered in the driveways as the priest repeated, "The Good Lord works in mysterious ways."

James Cooney sold his house and moved to Spain. A German with two Doberman Pinscher guard dogs was occasionally to be seen in the grounds of his mansion. The factory went to rack and ruin, excrement and empty beer bottles scattered about the once-thriving killing floor. Every bulb on the turret neon sign had been broken. The Sapphire Ballroom lay derelict and unsold, the paint peeling from the precious stone which hung precariously above the doorway where crudely-painted letters had been scrawled in the night: *Judas Cooney— Where are you now?*

The car traffic across the border ceased completely. Alec Hamilton sold up and moved away. In Pete's Pizza Parlour, Sergio folded napkins blankly, the jukebox unlit in the corner. The Turnpike Inn was purchased by two local brothers who turned it into a delicatessen, then a hairdresser's, then a turf accountants, then closed it down altogether. A minibus now left twice a week for the ferry terminals and airports of the major cities, picking up en route the latest batch of school leavers who waited with their sports bags and suitcases in every town along the way.

In the Railway Hotel, the few remaining youths and unemployed men played darts and scratched lottery tickets morosely. On the video screen above them, the crazed adolescent in the asbestos suit dragged the body of a screaming young girl into a freezer as the soundtrack blared. An old man sat transfixed beneath the screen, his terrified, perplexed eyes locked helplessly into every movement of the deranged youth. Two men in the corner argued bitterly about the actual date of the closure of the railway.

"It was 1959," said Francie Mohan without looking

away from the freezer where the adolescent was sharpening up a butcher's knife to desembowel the girl.

"What did I tell you?" said the man. "1959. Those were the days—what do you say Francie? The days before they closed the railway."

"Aye," replied Francie, "there was no stopping us then."

"The night they closed the railway—that was the night the clock stopped in the town of Carn. Oh I could tell you stories about this town . . ." The man stared into the well of his drink and faded off into a dreamy haze.

The girl on the screen screamed as a jet of blood splashed across the visor of the madman's asbestos suit. He raised the butcher's knife and brought it down in a sweeping arc with a maniacal laugh.

The barman began to sweep up the used lottery tickets. One of the youths cursed and swore to himself as he tore up yet another ticket and disappeared into the early afternoon.

"I remember the days when you couldn't move in this hotel for visitors. There were trains rolling into the station every half hour, packed with people. There were markets on the The Diamond every day—there was money to burn . . ."

The man shook his head. His drinking partner sighed wistfully. "Well there's one thing for sure—this town will never be the same again," he said, without looking up.

Francie Mohan finished his drink and slid down off the barstool. He pulled his greatcoat about him and said, "Don't worry. There's no need to worry."

The two men stared at him as he walked to the door. He turned and said, "There was a feast in the past and there'll be a feast in the future." They continued to stare blankly at him. Then he swung on his heel and shouted, "A feast of fuck-all," as the screams from the video screen floated out through the deserted foyer of the Railway Hotel.

On the mantelpiece of Sadie's bedroom, Josie Keenan smiled as she stood in a London street, behind her a flutter of pigeons. Around her ankles, in poor handwriting, the name *Gina Lollobrigida*.

Sadie visited the cemetery once a fortnight to say a small prayer for Josie by the gravestone that read,

Michael Joseph Keenan R.I.P.
Kathleen Josephine Keenan 1898–1946 R.I.P.

She stood on the hill overlooking the town. The church clock sounded the quarter hour. Through the streets Blast Morgan's son pushed a bin on two wheels. A carpet was beaten in a garden. The chickenhouse fan hummed. As on all those warm days years before, when she leaned over the fence at the bottom of his garden, Mr Galvin smiled at Sadie.

On it goes Sadie, and not a thing we can do about it. What was it you used to call them Sadie? The tick tock days of Carn? The tick tock days of Carn half a mile from the Irish border.

Mr Galvin smiled. Then he turned and went back to his ridges, prising at the clay with his garden fork as the sun beat down on him all those days ago.

He smiled again and then faded gently from her mind as he had passed from the earth.

On it goes Sadie, on it goes and not a thing we can do about it.

She took her daughter's hand and left the flowers on the grave. She walked back towards Abbeyville Gardens through the grounds of the church.

In the churchyard, many of the people of the town were on bended knee at the grotto of the Virgin Mary which had been built years before in the days of the railway to commemorate the Marian year. A rumour had circulated that she had been seen to move the night before. There was talk of her bringing a special sign to the town of Carn. The Virgin looked up at the whey-faced sky with a pale, chipped countenance. Beneath her pale feet, old women and middle-aged men fingered rosary beads anxiously. Beside them, in the fashionable black dress of their generation, freshfaced teenagers scanned the heavens hopefully. On the granite wall of the church Pat Lacey smiled, a framed portrait sponsored by the Anti-Divorce League. Beneath it, two small candles burned. The chant of the rosary began anew and they wrapped themselves in the arms of its consoling monotony, flickers of the past moving almost unseen across their minds, a tail of smog as a steam engine hissed into the depot, a flutter of coloured flags on Dolan Square, the music from The Sapphire spreading outward through the bustling, energetic streets.

But that was gone now and it was not for that they had come to the feet of the Virgin but for a sign that would take them back to the way it had been all those years ago, long before James Cooney, when there had been no questions to answer, when they had toiled long hours in the summer hayfields with the un-questioning acceptance of children, their sleep sound and undisturbed.

But a sign was not to come that evening and as Sadie made her way to Abbeyville Gardens, she saw them rise, heads still bowed, and like a silent wave, return to the empty streets where above on the hill, the rusting tower of the Carn Meat Processing Plant threw its evening shadow out across the huddled rooftops of the town.

8